Neighbours
of the Night

ENDRE ADY

Neighbours of the Night

~

Selected short stories

Selected, translated
and with a preface by

JUDITH SOLLOSY

CORVINA

Published in Hungary by Corvina Books, Ltd.
1051 Budapest, Vörösmarty tér 1, Hungary

This translation has been prepared
with the support of
the MTA-SOROS Foundation, Budapest

Design by Judit Kállói
Cover design by Judit Kállói

ISBN 963 13 3901 7

CONTENTS

CONTENTS

Preface

Endre Ady and Fin de Siècle Literature

Endre Ady (1877-1919), the renowned poet, writer, and journalist, worked for the papers all his life. In this he was not alone among his contemporaries; the progressive men of letters who in 1908 rallied around the new periodical pointedly called *Nyugat* (West) and who almost overnight shook Hungarian provincialism out of its self-contented slumber were, almost to the last man, contributors to the liberal newspapers.

In Hungary, where a burgeoning free middle class press played a formative role in the political and social life of the nation, belles lettres and journalism had long gone hand in hand. The papers gave generously of their pages to literature; most of Ady's poetry, too, first appeared in the dailies.

These dailies had another highly popular feature, the *tárca* or feuilleton story, so called to distinguish it from other forms of the genre, such as the longer novella. These were run at the bottom of the page every day, under the regular news articles. With just a couple of exceptions such as *The Kiss* (1908), which appeared in *Nyugat*, Ady's short stories, too, were written for the press. In one of his early pieces, *Ten Forints' Bridegroom* (1905), he describes one painful, personal aspect of this journal-dependent story-telling. But in the preface to the short story anthology *It Can Happen Like This* (1910), their author confesses that his stories were born of the urgency of thought and feeling that "wished to rid themselves of the jail house of verse." The Preface is here quoted in part.

> *This book is the chance meeting place of budding little histories, and I am beginning to regard it now as very much my own. (...) I gleaned its contents at random and as a sample from the skein of almost three-hundred of my newspaper novelettes. For sometimes it happened not merely from crude necessity or pecuniary imperative that my poems grew dissatisfied and wished to rid themselves of the jail house of verse, to see distant field through others' eyes – or at least with that intention. Besides, I wanted to show off, to prove that I can manage these too if I will. But now that they're together, I see only that I have gleaned a volume full from the many in a fortunate manner, and I feel only that this time I stand before those who read me, love me, loathe me or have grown accustomed to me, with poems in another guise... I believe that true music, true song, takes flight from where Death has his dominion. May those who respect Ady the poet hear issue from this book the song of reapers ambling home from the realm of Death. May they look kindly upon*

these [stories]... for after all, nothing happens in the world except what we feel, but that – that can happen like this.

In another place (a letter written from Paris to Antal Radó, editor of the series in which Ady's story anthology *Pale Men and Stories*, 1907, was to appear) he wrote:

I believe that a portion of my little feuilletons are, to a degree, documentary. I have treated new subjects... I have made attempts to enrich the form of the newspaper story or novelette, which has attained to such popularity in Hungary. To use a French word, I wished to add new frissons, to make this widely read, fashionable genre richer and more replete with ideas. Of course, I am perfectly aware of the serious shortcomings of these little novelettes. Write it down to my bent for over lyricizing on the one hand, and to the troublesome task of trailblazing on the other.

What makes Endre Ady's short stories so fascinating? Where lies their appeal?

Thanks partly to French (Zola and Maupassant) and partly to Russian (especially Turgenyev and Pushkin) inspiration, by the 1880s Naturalism and Symbolism began to appear in the works of Zoltán Ambrus, Sándor Bródy, Elek Gozsdú, Károly Lovik and others. And yet, in comparison to the writings of his predecessors and even contempraries, Ady's novelettes stand apart. This uniqueness owes a great deal to the felicitous conjoining of a predetermined disposition and sensibility, symbolic and lyrical, with a very special city – Paris, and an exciting new literature – the French, which gave it encouragement.

Between 1904 and 1911 Ady spent part of each year in the French capital, to be near his mistress. Léda, as Ady called her, was a well-educated woman of great personal charm, acquainted with many people of note in cultural life, and well versed in the new French literature. With her guidance Ady learned French and translated poems by Baudelaire and Verlaine. He also admired Mallarmé, Rimbaud and the other Symbolists in whose works he recognized a kindred spirit to the Secession, the Austro-Hungarian variant of art nouveau which he had first defended against the abuse of his provincialistic compatriots in an article back in 1899:

History has taught us [he wrote] that the bloodiest of transformations were born of the attempt of the self to free itself... Right now, this battle is waged ... in art and literature. The advocates of the old constraints hurl abuse at the apostles, misunderstand their efforts, and misunderstand, above all, what is at the heart of these efforts. The masses regard it as a fashion, whereas it is the first humble skirmish of a great universal transformation. Leave the Secession alone...! The Gibbons of the next century shall look back at this age from the new, transformed world of the Secession.

10

In Paris, Ady came face to face with a culture in which the struggle for unfettered individualism in the arts went hand in hand with long standing democratic tradition. For Ady, Paris was the city of light and of enlightenment, the breeding ground of revolutionary thought against which the near feudal conditions of his own homeland stood out in all the more glaring and painful relief. *Ten Forints' Bridgeroom* may have thought that he was merely courting the ten forints with the obligatory stories thrown down the insatiable gullet of whichever newspaper he happened to be working for. But even his earliest stories evidenced deep concern for the social contradictions of a country backward yet undergoing rapid development in its economic and political structure, a country where all this had little influence on the feudal conditions of the small towns and villages, and where, despite the growing proletarian movement and intellectual unrest, the lumbering state bureaucracy could not be stirred into action.

The other great catalyst for Ady's writings was his acquaintance with modern French literature, of which precious little was available in Hungarian translation. As he wrote in an article of 1906, "The new watchword is out: our artists must be kept away from accursed foreign parts, especially the West." But Ady, who by temperament had shared in the universal current of art nouveau even before he went to Paris, soon learned French and discovered the moderns for himself. Of course, this is not to imply sources and influences, but what is much more exciting, a shared spirit, sensibility and world view. For once the prose works of Ady, Géza Csáth, Victor Csolnoky, Dezső Szomori, Ernő Szép and others will be discovered abroad (and rediscovered at home), it will be seen that by the early years of the twentieth century Hungarian literature was very much part of a coherent Western tradition and that through its greatest representatives such as Ady, it shared in a core of common values. It is this background which helped create the special Ady prose that was once referred to as a revolt turned into a style. It is a prose expressing new themes through a sometimes high strung, ecstatic and symbolic manner, the recourse to unexpected metaphors and linguistic neologisms, all so characteristic of the fin de siècle feuilleton. The erotic fuses with the political, the personal with the social; there is an uncompromising drive to take words by the throat, the bold and scathing clashing with the almost embarrassingly frank and personal.

For Ady, this power of the word to create new worlds and meanings went hand in hand with the preoccupation of the Symbolists to obliterate the abyss separating life and art. The last decades of the 19th century found themselves face to face with the discovery of subjectivity and its consequence, a world become fragmented, knowable only in parts. In this fragmented universe, the artist appeared as a sovereign creator who, as Oscar Wilde said, could make Life imitate Art.

Endre Ady's feeling, too, in his short stories at least, was that life follows art, which in turn seems so real and intense that it leads to madness, or worse, as in *Neighbours of the Night* and *The Blinded Muse*. In another story, to me one of this most remarkable, he addressed himself to the unresolved and unresolvable conflict between the sexes, another prominent Symbolist preoccupation. Entitled *Bond and the Spider of Old Age* (1905), it raises the popular art nouveau theme to tragic heights as the cult of the self calls for the kind of in-depth scrutiny that drags deep-rooted instincts into the blinding light of consciousness. Ady probed within his own self with the boldness and acumen that anticipated the discoveries of psyshoanalysis.

As in all his stories, words are used in unexpected ways and in unexpected juxtapositions, thus commanding our attention and lending new authenticity to meaning, while the at times ambiguous syntax contributes to the sense of unity that pervades the whole. Images jostle each other for room, then flit away. We feel as though we could catch the act of creation and self-absorption in the making. We feel a hidden, more essential reality behind the appearances, whether we think of Ady's wildest and most self-indulgent art nouveau pieces such as *Thomas in the Red Garden*, *The Mute Couple* and *Flora*, or such subtle, Thomas Mann like works as *The Ghost of Rachel Szelezsán* and *The Sensitive Lieutenant*. Like Rimbaud, Ady filled nature with new meaning, using symbols to unveil the underlying mystery of life.

But unlike Rimbaud, Ady made no effort to escape from the limits of Self, nor did he see the human condition as quite so fleeting. Yet for him, too, the turn of the century style we call Decadence, Symbolism or Secession was synonymous with non-conformity. It was not only a style, but a liberation from style, not only a style, a sensibility, a way of life or a movement, but all of these at once.

Judith Sollosy

Hoeing the Beet

On the five-thousand acre Batáry estate the girls worked for thirty krajcárs a day. They hoed the beet and sang, for it was May, when the young blood stirs to life. From time to time a stripling of an overseer rode out to them, running sweetly at the mouth as he glared at their ripe forms. He would have to amuse himself with them, but he was afraid they would laugh at him. Besides, Tom Batáry might show up at any time. The old man was like a regular romany; led by his two dapple greys, he wandered around his lands at all hours of the day.

Jusztina busied herself at the head of the girls. It was she who broke into a new song whenever with a sigh or two, they had finished the old. Besides, Jusztina might have had something of the gentlefolk in her. A peasant girl of landless nobles of whom there are so many around our part of the country-side, wide-hipped, ruddy-cheeked, full-bosomed, she may have even been distantly related to the Batárys. Further in the back hoed the two gypsy girls, Petyka and Juliska. But unlike the others, they did not sing. The other girls would have nothing to do with them, even though they all worked for just thirty krajcárs a day.

Old man Batáry showed up with the two dapple greys at noon. He called for the young overseer, who was idling around on his horse by the beet field. The old man chided the overseer, for the girls were not hoeing well. But once he had spent his anger in this manner, he was congenial once more. He strolled over to the girls, who were at their midday meal.

"Jusztina! Jusztina Bakos!"

Jusztina rose from her meal and swinging her hips lightly, walked over to this lordship.

"Well, Jusztina. What's new?"

"The two gypsies give us no end of trouble, your worship."

Old man Batáry shouted for the two gypsy girls.

"Hey, you, gypsies! What's their name? Oh, yes. Petyka! Juliska!"

The two gypsy girls walked up to old man Batáry. They were more dead than alive, but it was only right and proper that they should be doing the lion's share of the work.

Tom Batáry eyed them with pleasure. Petyka and Juliska were smooth-skinned and pleasantly plum and had such pretty eyes, too. But his worship turned back to Jusztina just the same.

"Well. What's the complaint against them?"

Jusztina bristled with indignation.

"These gypsies want to drink from our jug!"

16

Tom Batáry looked at the two gypsy girls with genuine wonder.

"Well, well... Is this true, Petyka?"

Petyka was the older and also the more forward of the two; besides, his worship had addressed her, so she was the one to speak.

"It is true. We are all girls here. We all work for thirty krajcárs a day. Our lips are as clean as theirs. But to our shame, they bring us separate jugs. Well, we won't have it! We want to drink from theirs."

Tom Batáry scratched his head, then motioned to the stripling overseer.

"Overseer! Have four or five big jugs of water brought out here in the morning. Let the girls have their pick."

But Pletyka cut him short.

"That won't do, your worship," she said brashly. "We want to drink from the same jug as the others."

Jusztina chuckled. His lordship fell to thinking. Such good-looking girls. And he could have them do anything for him. Besides, they could always be relied upon to come as field hands for just thirty krajcárs a day. But the others outnumbered them. He needed them more. This was no time to dispense justice. Better leave that to the overseer.

"Overseer, see that something is done. Jusztina, make sure the girls work. Whoever slacks off now won't get to hoe the new corn."

Tom Batáry mounted his buggy and had himself driven off. The girls went back to work, with the two gypsies hoeing off to the side as before. The others wouldn't even hoe in the same group with them. The girls sweated and suffered, but they sang all the same. They had to hurry so they could finish their appointed patch by nightfall.

Petyka and Juliska nearly perished from thirst. In the morning and at noon, they drank from the trough. No matter how thirsty they were, they refused to touch the jug set aside for them. They were Tom Batáry's hired hands, same as the others. They were girls, too, and young, just like them.

The other girls concealed their jug in a nearby grove, and as they sang, they laughed at the misery of the two gypsy girls. They were beggars, every one of them. They lived on bread and a slice of stale bacon. When at the end of the week they received their hire, three times what they got wouldn't have sufficed to pay their debts. It was a blessing, besides, if come Sunday, the father of one or another of the girls didn't drink her money away. But they were proud, and that made them feel good. On Sundays, they walked humbly to the Batáry mansion for their hire, but they'd go separately even then, never with the two gypsies.

However, on this particular day in May, the girls did not return to the village, for come five in the morning, they would have to resume work anyway. The village was a ways off, besides, while the night was warm and lovely.

Petyka and Juliska made separate sleeping quarters for themselves at a good distance from the others. They did not sing, but they could not sleep either. It was late, and the silence all-pervasive. It must have been around midnight when Petyka spoke up at last.

"Juliska, come with me!"

Together, they headed on tiptoes for the grove and began their search without a sound. They searched everything thoroughly, and at great length. They found the jug at last, swaddled in green sedge. Carefully, Petyka removed the sedge, then drank as if it were not water she was drinking but life, happiness, the fulfilment of her dreams.

"Juliska, it's your turn!"

And Juliska drank, too, deeply and devoutly. When she had drunk her fill, they swaddled up the jug again, though it was nearly empty.

In the morning, the rest of the girls went to get their jug, and as they did so, they giggled. "Nobody has touched it. No gypsy is going to drink out of this!" And with beaming faces, they picked up their hoes in order to toil for the salvation of their worships the Batárys for thirty krajcárs a day. But on this particular morning, the gypsy girls were happy, too, at last.

This, then, is the way beet is hoed in our glorious Hungary.

1906

19

The Justice of the Óhidys

Once there was a county in Transylvania, and in this county there was a village where the tough-minded Óhidys had been living in a towered mansion for many long years. No one ever gave them serious offence, and they always bargained successfully with the German, the Turk, their neighbours, even princes. They kept a close watch over their serfs, and by the grace of a so-called Providence, prospered. Their highnesses became counts of a large imperial estate. But their ancestors had been some sort of Italian vagabonds, and their adventurer's blood would often stir them to action. And so, they continued strong and handsome, and the terrors of the countryside, even to this day, when Louis Kossuth has long since turned to dust.

For the Óhidys would malign Kossuth himself.*

They watched the swift chariot of time pass by with obdurate minds. Foaming at the mouth, they railed against change and kept an unflinching eye on their Hungarian and Romanian cotters lest some strange new fancy work them harm. This, then, is how they lived, following in their ancestors' footsteps. Such a thing is conceivable only in Hungary or China. In these lands, time flies by without shedding a feather. These countries still belong to the mandarins. We, the common people, come into this world and are humbled; we serve our appointed time, shed our quota of tears and die. Such is our lot, while life belongs to the Óhidys, along with everything else – rank, mandate, trust, popularity, the creatures of the woods, the fish of the waters, and the impoverished maidens, too – the maidens especially!

Mischievous banter had been making the rounds of the Transylvanian countryside for two-hundred years. The tyrant Óhidys had amorous dispositions, and so, on the Óhidy estate, each face mirrors the next. No maiden's honour was safe from them. Nor were they averse to irregular marriages. At the

---

*Like many other aristocrats, the Óhidys were given their lands and titles not from the king, but from the Holy Roman Empire, which until 1806 was ruled by the Austrian House of Habsburg. Thus, the Óhidys would have been natural enemies of Louis Kossuth (1802-1894), who inspired Hungary's struggle for independence from Austria and led the ill-fated anti-Habsburg uprising of 1848-1849.

beginning of the last century, for instance, a notorious Óhidy count had acknowledged thirty-nine illegitimate offspring. The family stood firm, however, and the court ruled in its favour. The old count was declared insane, and the fortune remained mercifully intact in the hands of the legitimate Óhidys. For the family was legitimate up to Ádám Óhidy, who had shared the inherited wealth with his two brothers. Then one of the brothers loved himself sick in Paris and wasted away in his youth, while the other got himself embroiled in a trifling matter of cards at the National Casino, which in turn led to his death. And so, Count Ádám found himself sole heir.

Count Ádám procured himself a wife from Vienna, a creature of Czech-German extraction. The Czech-German countess was wealthy and high born, and so the marriage of the only surviving Óhidy could have been a happy one, were it not for the fact that the new Countess brought her manservant with her, a Czech lad, a big, strong good-for-nothing boy with hair as yellow as bad saffron.

But Count Ádám's marriage was blessed. Providence would not stand by and suffer such an illustrious family as the Óhidys to die out. And so, the tiny counts and countesses came in quick succession. The only trouble was that they had yellow hair, whereas the Óhidys have always regarded the world with Italian gypsy complexions and bright, raven eyes. Study the ancestral portraits in the Óhidy mansion; take a good look at each and every one of them.

They are all like this, without exception. The Óhidys even chose their brides in their own image.

No matter. Count Ádám did not seem to mind. He was not of a jealous disposition. And after all, isn't that what counts? When he joined the bosom of his ancestors, he did so in peace. He had at least five grandchildren by then, and four sons, too. The Óhidy line would survive...

What follows happened not so long ago. After Count Ádám passed away, his eldest son, Count Félix, took charge of the estate. This Count Félix had a Czech countenance and an unbridled, brutal nature. For wildness is not a matter of blood. Like anyone else, manservants, too, can sneak cockoo eggs into the nests of blue-bloods. That is no reason for the ancestors to blush and stir uneasy in their graves. Even bastards can prove worthy of them.

By the way, Count Ádám's wife was still alive, and the Czech manservant, too, who was a very old man by then. Félix would have driven the old fellow off long ago, perhaps because he suspected the role he had played in the latest chapter of the Óhidy family history. He hated the fellow, his father; but because of his mother, he held his peace.

Otherwise, life's river ran its appointed course. The countryside belonged to Count Félix, its reigning monarch, and he was determined to be worthy of the Óhidy name to which (truth to tell) he had precious little right.

Then one springtime, a strange contagion swept through the county of the Óhidys. Just before harvest, the descendants of the serfs held secret gatherings. Hungarian and Romanian peasants began saying the most outrageous things. Like it won't do, thousands living for the benefit of a handful of people who inhabit the towered mansion – if you can call it living at all, when every winter decimates the starving. And so, they demanded more compassion from the inhabitants of the towered mansion.

What audacity! If he had his way, Count Félix would have liked to order a couple of cannon and massacre the whole lot of rebelling slaves. But who would do the work then? Who would reap? And so, Count Félix resorted to bargaining instead. Curbing his rage, he made a string of promises. By the end of the harvest, though, he thought better of it. He told his bailiffs, "Go and whip the peasants and tell them not to expect more hire than their fathers and grand-fathers had before them."

Then one day in July, messengers came running. Those rascals, the peasants, refused to cut down the wheat. They had straightened out their hoes and were marching on the towered mansion.

Luckily, the old manservant had his wits about him. "Have some men ride to the chief constable and the police. We will not allow this thing!"

"We will not allow this thing," echoed Count Félix after the old manservant, his father.

The police came just in the nick of time, and they came in great numbers. A half an hour more, and it might have been too late. But they opened fire right away. How many died? Twenty? Thirty? What's the difference? They were wretched peasants, every one of them! Frightened, the survivors took to their heels to resume the harvest the next day, proof sufficient that it was no use, rebelling against their lordships.

The chief constable took a proud survey of the battlefield. Behind him came the Count's family and the old manservant. They looked at the faces of the dead. A wonderful thing – they all resembled the ancient portraits hanging in the Óhidy mansion. The rebels had all been Óhidys. They wanted an extra piece of bread, and now they lay bloody and slain.

It was the old manservant who delivered their epitaph: "It served the bastards right."

1906

Joba the Stone Crusher

Joba the stone crusher was wandering about town,*
where flags fluttered atop snow-clad roofs. He was
hungry. He cracked his knuckles, which were gnarled,
sore and blue, and cursed as he followed in the wake
of the rushing crowd. In this manner he soon found
himself standing in front of the ornate palace gate, and
as the people poured through the ornate gate, Joba
thought he must be dreaming. Could he really be
allowed in among the flowers and the gentle fawns?
What manner of bewitchment was this on a strange
winter morn? He'd watched, oh, how often he'd
watched this garden of miracles from a humble distance, its white paths, its flowers, its gentle fawns, and
the towered palace set in the middle of the grounds.
And oh, could that be a gypsy band playing inside?

*The story is set in Nagybánya, where the Károlyi counts, who
owned most of the town, lived in an anachronistic medieval-style
palace with seven towers set in the middle of an immense park.
Inspiration for the story came from the elections of 1901, when in
accordance with custom, the aristocracy and nobility attempted
to win votes by opening their homes to the common people.

Meanwhile, the crowd had thickened. Some were in rags. Joba watched from outside the gate with great, sickly, helpless amazement. A group of the ragged ones rushed past him. One of them saw Joba and called to him as he darted past, "Well, if that ain't Joba of Csege! Come along, if ye be a true patriot!"

When he heard the strains of the Kossuth Song,* Joba made something like a light-hearted move. He made up his mind to go inside with the rest. Besides, the man who had hailed him was from Bencs, and a stone crusher, like himself. Something of great import must be happening inside, he felt, if such a princely mansion was willing to put up with the likes of him upon its grounds.

Joba ran where the lad from Bencs was racing with his fellows, right to the front of the many-towered mansion. The immense park echoed and reechoed with the sound of people singing. From the palace windows bright, friendly faces beamed down at them. A piece of heaven, Joba the stone crusher thought as he allowed the sun to warm his back.

The melting snow sparkled. People's ears were turning crimson. From time to time, cheers rent the air, and behatted townswomen waved their shawls. Joba the stone crusher reeled as if he'd been drinking home-made *pálinka*. He cheered along, he laughed and hummed – he had, indeed, almost forgotten to groan.

*The Kossuth Song, born during the freedom fights against Habsburg domination (1848-1849), remained a patriotic song for many decades to come.

28

The men of shreds and patches were huddled together in the back of the crowd. Joba recognized many of them, and he smiled. Ditch diggers from Bencs, basket weavers from Lápfalu, tenant farmers from Vadág, stray hands, breadless stone crushers, they had all huddled in a group, unawares.

Just prior to the approach of spring, such as in February, sleeping villages are stirred to life with a cry of pain. The people have had enough of winter, and like sleepwalkers, begin to drift into town. They don't know why they obey the summons, but obey they do. There are handsome houses in town, money, expensive things, work, bread, and hope. And so they come, the pallid, the bitter, the ragged, the starved. This is why they came, too, the people of Bencs, of Lápfalu and Vadág, and all the rest. This is why Joba had come into town himself, he who was singing now like one intoxicated. He sobbed as he sang the gypsies' song: *"Kossuth Lajos azt üzente"**. The entire rent, emaciated, ragged hoard were singing, "Long live the homeland! Long live the homeland!"

"And now we're all here, on equal footing, in the Count's garden," Joba thought. He'd had a dream just like this the other day, when he was on the verge of death. His lungs were still inflamed. He had suf-

*The opening line of the Kossuth Song, the first stanza of which runs: "Lajos Kossuth has sent us word / He's run short of his regiment. / Should he send us word again / Off we must go to the last man. / Long live our liberty! / Long live our homeland!"

fered for weeks, and it had been just five days since he'd hauled himself up from the hot straw mat where he'd lain. He could still feel the pain, like the repeated stabbing of a knife, and he was still prone to light-headedness, besides. His rags, too, were thin and wretched.

In the midst of the commotion a tenant farmer from Vadág edged over to his side.

"You're looking poorly, friend."

Because of the gypsies, the song and the jubilation, they could hardly hear each other. Besides, they both felt giddy from the unaccustomed crowds.

"I was nearly a gonner, friend. They were about to lay me out. And I wish they had. There's no work in the village. And I'd be unfit for it anyhow. I came to town to look around. Is it the same with you in Vadág? My wife's near death's door herself. Been sickly a fortnight."

"Got any little ones?"

"Five. I haven't got an appetite, at least. I have no appetite for life. But they eat plenty. What's a body to do?"

Presently, their voices were drowned out by a mighty uproar. The crowd cheered because the young Count appeared at the window.

The farmer from Vadág whispered reverentially. "He'll be our man in Parliament now, after his old man."

The Count's speech was short, but oh, so exquisite! All men should be happy and free, he said. And when he concluded, the townswomen waved their shawls again. And again, Joba's eyes filled with tears. Then the Count's servants herded the crowd off the grounds. It was past noon by then. But for some time yet, the gypsies' song could still be heard: *"Kossuth Lajos azt üzente..."*

Joba continued to hum light-heartedly as he walked along with the farmer from Vadág. But then, he began to shiver.

"I can't go home like this. Not like this. If only I could buy a loaf of bread. I am going to get bread. And I am going to get meat."

Joba felt a great change coming over the world. Such a strange morning... The Count's park... The Count... The music... The prolonged cheering... And everybody together as one, the high and the low. There must be meat to be had, and bread, too, Joba thought as fever and hope fired his countenance.

"I've got some money, friend. I sold two piglets," the farmer from Vadág said. "Let's have a drink."

And they drank until sunset. They wept and they sang, *"Kossuth Lajos azt üzente"*. Over and over again, the farmer from Vadág shrilled, "A new world is dawning, friend! All men will be free, the devil take it!"

Joba wept like a child. "I'd like to kiss that young Count. He's a blessed sort, I tell you, a blessed sort!" And they sang as if in anticipation of the happiness to come, *"Kossuth Lajos azt üzente"*.

It was night by the time they started for home, with nothing but the white reflection of the snow to show the way. Seeing that the farmer from Vadág still had five forints left, Joba said, "Friend, could you spare a forint."

"I can't," said the other.

When the staggering farmer passed him, Joba struck him over the head with his club. Then, when the man was down, he went berserk. Every bone in his body shrilled as he repeatedly struck the man over the head. Then he took the five forints from his boots and broke into a run across the deserted, dark, and wintry field. He was singing *"Kossuth Lajos azt üzente"*, and his heart was fired with the day's events as he headed home with the five forints, like the redeemed king of a fairy tale.

1906

Béni the Apostle

Béni, the six-year-old apostle, was ravished by a blissful fever one night. He knew whom he would make happy on the morrow. He was up by dawn, thinking of Lenci, whose father was a gravedigger, and who lived on the outskirts of town. Lenci's father was always coughing – coughing away and slugging down *pálinka*. He thrashed Lenci, who had five other brothers and sisters, regularly. But Lenci was a ragged, devil-may-care, cheerful lad. In winter he wore home-made moccasins, but they were amply lined with rags, so he didn't care. And once, at a wake, he'd tasted hot food, even meat.

Béni had to sneak out because he was being watched. He sneaked through the small garden gate and headed for the outskirts over the open countryside. As the mischievous March air was tugging at his lungs he was panting a little, and under his fine, translucent skin, his blood was playing hide and seek. Besides, he was carrying a heavy load, a large paper box laden with precious goods. His pockets were bulging, too. He looked up. In the far,

far distance glistened the white Bózsa Mound. Béni was elated. They, Lenci and he, would be going up there soon to pick snow flowers.

The outskirts were at a good distance, but Lenci came part of the way to meet him. He was barefoot, and as he advanced, he bopped up and down like a half-crazed squirrel. He was decked out in the top half of one of his father's old, rancid-smelling hats, with a bright cock's feather stuck in its side. His reddish-brown, unwashed cheeks gleamed, though his father must have thrashed him in the morning, for tiny tear-rivulets were embedded in his skin. This face, it was like a map. But it was a cheerful face, too, and the rays of the sun danced merrily upon it.

"Well, what have you brought, Béni?"

Béni smiled a wise, benevolent smile. Then with profound gravity, he proceeded to reveal the most important piece of news first.

"Meat. Good ham. Red ham."

"Did they see you?"

"No."

"What else?"

"I took twenty coins from the money box. And I brought the hat I wore last year, and two oranges, and a big piece of chocolate. But give some of it to your brother Gyuri, all right? And there's also an embroidered shawl for your mother, and fragrant water."

However, Lenci was growing impatient.

"What about shoes? Sunday last, you gave shoes to the gypsy Lajkó, over at the Kovácses."

"He was coughing. Besides, they hide my shoes. They watch me very closely. I had a hard time sneaking away. Are we going up to the Bózsa Mound? Are we? Let's go before they catch up with me!"

Lenci shrugged. He looked out of sorts. He ran ahead with the things, probably to hide them. Then they set out for the Bózsa Mound. But as they walked, Lenci spoke in sad, cunning tones.

"You have everything you need, when I never even tasted a slice of bread and butter in all my life."

Béni's heart trembled with sympathy. The reproach stung him. He cleared his throat.

"Bread and butter is no good," he said softly. "I always give mine to the hired hand's son. I never eat bread and butter."

They continued walking. The climb involved a lot of detours, as springtime puddles were everywhere. But the Bózsa Mound waited, glistening, up ahead. Only Lenci's mood of sadness would not let up.

"The bur weed never pricks your feet. You even got socks that reach up to your knees. You're always wearing shoes."

"I'd like to pull them off and go barefoot. But I'm not allowed. The other day I pulled them off in the garden, and Mademoiselle saw, and I got no dinner."

"But you have more than twenty coins in your money box. They never give me any money!"

By the time they reached the Bózsa Mound, Béni was feeling feeble and flushed. He sat down on the green grass next to some patch of snow. He was wheezing, and this frightened him, because he had

35

to spend a very long time in bed once before when the same thing had happened.

The two boys descended the slope, where the sun shone as brightly as if it were summer. The snow flowers, too, were in bloom. Béni was overjoyed. But then he began to cough. The sun disappeared, and the Bózsa Mound became wrapped in mist. The sky turned leaden, and the village could hardly be seen.

"Let's go home, Lenci," Béni pleaded. But Lenci, who was squatting on the ground with his head on his bare, strong, grimy knees, refused to budge. Whimpering, Béni called to him again. He was scared. Oh, what will happen? They're probably having dinner already. And what if it should start to rain? He was on the verge of tears.

"Let's go home, Lenci! What's the matter with you, Lenci?"

"I want shoes. You have so many shoes. And I want a hat just like yours. Blue, fine, and with a long ribbon. I want some shoes, and I want a hat!"

"You'll have them tomorrow."

Lenci fell silent. The time passed, and the sky turned darker still. What will they do to him, Béni thought, anxious and despairing. He was trembling, but he felt sorry for Lenci, too. Poor boy, he looked so disconsolate. He'd have gladly given Lenci all he had, just to make him stop crying, because Lenci was crying in full earnest, he was lying on the ground, and the wet grass was staining his cheeks.

"I never had shoes!" he sobbed. "I never had a hat!"

"Wait till tomorrow."

"I want them now!"

The rain began to pelt them. It was sleety rain. Béni sat down on the ground and pulled off his shoes. Lenci bound the little shoes with a piece of string and flung them over his shoulder.

"And now, your hat!"

Béni handed him his hat, too.

There was no avoiding the puddles as they ran towards the village. From time to time, the melting snow reached up to their knees. Béni's teeth chattered. He felt hot and cold all over. He would have liked to lie down in the melting snow.

As they reached the upper end of the village, he turned to Lenci.

"Give me the shoes and the hat until tomorrow. I can't go home like this. You can have them back tomorrow. I'll bring you bread and butter, too. I'll take more money out of the money box. I'll even give you a pair of patent leather boots. I'm so cold!"

As he swung the shoes triumphantly on the string, Lenci whistled a cheerful tune. In the other hand, he was waving the hat. The rain pelted his cheeks, but he pranced about merrily. A thousand sleets couldn't harm him. He was like a diminutive meadow deity – pagan, high-spirited, grimy, strong. He splashed about in the puddles as if Béni wasn't even there any more, and he sprinted ahead. Just once, though, he looked back.

"God bless you, Béni," he said. "And don't tell them what you did with the shoes and hat. You're a good boy. You can come with me again tomorrow!"

37

The praise gratified Béni. But he was shaken by a heavy fit of coughing. He couldn't even say good bye to Lenci. Oh, what will happen when they ask? He's going to tell a lie. And lying is bad. But what is he to do? He's going to throw away the snow flower he was holding in this hand, for one thing. And for another, he's going to say that some wandering gypsies grabbed him out in the fields and took his shoes and hat. Otherwise, Lenci might get into trouble, and Lenci was a good boy. Besides, his father thrashed him a lot. Poor Lenci, he had nothing to call his own.

When he reached home, Béni was put to bed. For the next ten days he was delirious. He could not take Lenci his bread and butter. And when the ten days were up, he died.

1906

The Sensitive Lieutenant

From the remote, hilly quarter of the army camp opposite, the two men could clearly hear the plaintive songs of the Hungarian soldiers drifting in their direction. Sitting apart, they were engaged in a childish dispute without rhyme, reason, or conviction. It was a lovely, intense Sunday afternoon in early summer. But what good was such a Sunday afternoon to two rugged men in war-torn Bosnia?* And what good was it to anyone if two gentlemen, the engineer Mr Papp and the lieutenant Mr Rubek, had put their head together, intent on unravelling the mystery of life?

"No doubt," said Rubek with a yawn, "life is truly the primary, the most serious, the most thoroughly real thing of all. We should give life its due. But beyond life looms death, don't forget. Besides, living takes women and money." And he sighed.

*Not content with its own territories, in June 1878 the Austro-Hungarian Monarchy took advantage of the aftermath of the 1875 Serbian uprising against Turkish domination and the subsequent Russo-Turkish war to occupy Bosnia and Hercegovina.

"Maybe I should go check on my railway," the blonde, paunchy engineer sighed in turn as he eyed the improvised canteen for the hundredth time.

The smell of blood had lifted from the vicinity of the camp by then, but there was still bad news coming from outlying areas. The restlessness was considerable, the mood of the men unsteady and gloomy, the camp regulations rigorous and depressing.

Papp, the peace-loving engineer, was no longer a soldier, but he was detained in the army to help lay the rails. This work was almost as important as the killing; let this barbaric hoard see that blessed miracle of civilisation, the railroad! But all told, the most distressing thing about the place was that there could be no talk of women or of love. Or rather, there could be nothing but talk, and once the talk had turned wistful and pained, philosophy invariably followed.

"I'll come along, if you don't mind," said Papp's friend, Lieutenant Rubek, who was very restless by then.

Papp's railway was a short, barely begun affair that clambered up a woody hillside. On such a god awful, sweltering afternoon, this walk promised to bring much-needed relief to the two melancholy men. They were old pals who hailed from the same town and who, even as youngsters, enjoyed a good argument despite the fact that they never entertained a very high opinion of each other. They would have gone mad, perhaps, had not fate brought them together like this in Bosnia to continue the old carefree, inconsequential debates.

40

"What I'd like to know," Rubek stammered as they set out for the woods, "is where these bastards hide their women. Or why, if we happen to run into them, we must treat them like wealthy aunts holding an inheritance over our heads."

"If women were free pray," the mild tempered Papp laughed, "the soldiers couldn't kill as efficiently. Our generals are top-notch psychologists, believe me. They know what they're about. Deprivation in love turns a healthy male into a first-rate killing machine. Just what we need right now."

"What we need right now," Rubek retorted, "is for cynics like yourself not to pollute God's precious air!"

Though the gallant Rubek was not really annoyed, he had no particular sympathy for or understanding of these principles of his friend. He, Rubek, loathed those filthy lips that besmirched the fondest values in life. "For instance," he often thought during these difficult days, "take this podgy, meek faced civilian, this engineer. He boasts that he's a man of culture, refinement, and progress, yet he thinks that life is nothing but filth."

Lieutenant Rubek was a poet of sorts, fond of beautifying earthly things, a man who took great pride in the refinement of this soul. In war, however, he took no delight at all, being inordinately fond of his precious and well groomed hide. But some things he held in high esteem all the same: courage, the perilous flirtation with death, the noble goals which those in high places surely understood better than himself. Rubek despised those who defiled beautiful things and explained everything away with recourse to the appetite, wealth, and the gross need for love.

"Nevertheless," murmured the engineer who had grown tired of the conversation once again and so turned a critical eye on his railway bed, "the generals are right, not wanting the men to go chasing after women at a time like this. Killing is of the essence so this thing can end with the utmost dispatch, and war is expensive. It is waged for profit."

The lieutenant would not even vouchsafe a reply. Had he not known better, he could have sworn that the engineer was a Jew. Lieutenant Rubek had no liking for Jews and resented this insult in the name of the entire army corps. To say a thing like this, that war is waged for profit, for gain, phew! And this Papp a soldier still in a way!

They perspired as they stumbled along the railway bed. The woods had been cleared in spots, and all the heat seemed to be trapped in these small clearings.

Suddenly, they heard a blast. Lieutenant Rubek screamed, jumped into the air three times, shook himself, then felt his body all over for injury. So pale that he was almost white, Papp stopped in his tracks. With steady hands he pulled out his huge revolver. There came a second blast, then the whistle of a bullet, like before, but a few seconds later it was Papp who pulled the trigger, and barely eight steps from where they stood, a man roared. It was an old

Muslim, sixty-five years of age, distinguished of dress, and dead. Papp had a sharp eye and a steady hand, and the poor old bastard reached his Maker in a flash.

"Let's head back," suggested Papp in subdued tones. "We've had quite enough excitement for one day. I'm going home to work."

"You've just killed a poor old fanatic and you want to go back to your desk?"

"Naturally. Drawing and making calculations are the best tranquillizers I know. Besides, I'm no miracle worker to raise the old gentleman from the dead."

Rubek turned on him. "You bastard! Why did you have to shoot him?" he asked, hardly able to control himself.

"Because if I give him time, he kills me. Or you. You love life, which you find so poetic, and as for me, my mother expects me back from Bosnia. Besides, we're both still quite young."

Papp was very angry. He started briskly back to camp along the railway bed. He was in no mood to talk; he did not even glance behind him. He had had quite enough for one day, even of the lieutenant's company. He worked a little, but did not visit the canteen, for he did not wish to see Rubek again that day, and retired early.

A highly welcome, cool, sleep-inducing nigh came, but Papp had hardly dropped off to sleep when someone woke him.

It was Lieutenant Rubek. As he made some light in the engineer's wooden shack, he looked pale and unsteady on his feet, as if he'd been drinking.

"What do you want?" the paunchy, blonde engineer barked, irate yet stunned with sleep. And he yawned.

"I've got a small fortune on me, and half of it, at least, is yours by right, if you want it."

"But where did you get all that money, enough to get drunk on?"

"I... I...," stammered Rubek, "I went back to the old man."

"So you went back. That's your business. And if you found money on him, that's your business, too. Keep it. Such is war. Keep the money. It's yours. And you know that I can keep my mouth shut."

Lieutenant Rubek dared not look the engineer in the eye, and so made a move to go.

"I... I'd like to give all this money to the first woman I run into worth her salt. I'd give her my pay, too. Six months' worth."

"Fine, fine," yawned the blonde engineer. "But I'm awfully sleepy, and you go to the devil!"

Somewhere in the army camp, a handful of Hungarian privates were singing a sad song filled with longing, filled with love. It was against regulations to sing at this time of the night, but they were singing for them all, and surely, no hurt would come to them in consequence.

1910

The Ghost of Rachel Szelezsán

They carried it past my window yesterday, four young men carried the blue coffin of Rachel Szelezsán in knee-deep mud. On Monday she received a letter from her sweetheart in America; he's had enough of starvation, she should help him return. Rachel had nothing but her white complexion, fine body, slender grace, and youthful twenty years.

She began to weep, by nightfall was shivering, on Tuesday was still able to leave her bed, by Wendesday talked a great deal, but without sense, on Thursday they applied leeches under her two firm, feverish breasts, on Friday her body was covered with spots, and on Saturday, in keeping with custom, she was laid in a blue coffin. There was no money for a doctor, but the spring mud would have engulfed a hundred carts and a hundred doctors around the parts where I live in any case. Rachel was buried on Sunday afternoon.

The whole village mourned because she was young and pretty, and if she took on odd jobs, the work veritably burnt up under her hands. Everyone swore then that it was worry that killed her, no matter how spotted her body might have been. Just twenty years ago, such dramatic cases of scarlet fever would have served as the stuff of song. But now, the parish priest appeared half-heartedly enough, for he could expect only a meagre dole – and he was covered with mud besides. He grumbled, recited something, and cast uneasy glances at the sky, where dark clouds gathered overhead. By the time they reached my window, the ugly spring tempest was howling in earnest. The rain poured from the black clouds and washed the fresh blue paint from the blue coffin. Half the village was there in the procession, the parish priest up front, like some black, drenched devil. We watched this with something like satisfaction, old Toma Jepura and I.

Toma Jepura lives across from us, at the end of the village. He is a good-for-nothing old drunkard, but he is wise; perhaps that is why he lives here, by the graveyard, just like me. And because Toma Jepura and I live by the graveyard, we are past wondering at many things that still make others wonder, especially Jepura, who digs graves when he finds nothing better to occupy his time, and when he deems the amount of *pálinka* sufficient. Besides, why shouldn't he be digging graves, seeing how close he lives to the graveyard?

In short, the two of us, Jepura and I, are the kind of folk who see beyond the village, and even a little beyond this life of vanity. We have never spoken to each other, Jepura and I, but we keep an eye out for each other, and perhaps it will not be taken amiss if I add that we do so with affection. We have seen many a burial in our time, we have dug many a grave, old Jepura with a shovel, I by other means. That he is more ragged than I, has seen less of the world, can neither read nor write – this is of consequence only to the weak-minded. Neither Jepura nor I are nearly as perfect as we think, just that there is less frailty in us than in those living further removed from the graveyard. We are no proof against the power of ailment, for one thing, the lure of drink, the weather, money, and women. I have no wife, at least, but Jepura, whom the Romanian priest in our village calls Jepuré, in the Oláh manner,* has a lawfully wedded wife. This woman has grown old, whereas a wise man who likes his liquor carries something of his youth with him to the grave.

They buried Rachel Szelezsán on Sunday, in frightful weather, but by Monday, this crazy March was all aglitter. We woke to such a spring, to such sweet unrest, as if it were June at the very least. I glanced out the window. Across on the porch, Toma Jepura lay exposing his belly to the blesed sun. He had untied the string that held an old, cast-off, buttonless gentleman's coat around his waist. He even pulled his shirt out from under it; after its winter fast, let his belly have its fill of sunshine.

*'Oláh' was the epithet by which the Hungarians of western Hungary (Transylvania) called the Romanians living among them.

47

But Toma Jepura's ancient, bearded, unkempt face shone so bright, I had a premonition that something would go amiss.

At three in the afternoon, Jepura was still warming himself on the porch. He had not even eaten, perhaps; wise men rarely make much ado about their victuals. He was holding a willow twig in his hand, and was merrily beating the receding mud with it. I could see by his expression that he would have preferred to play gidde'ap and ride around a bit brandishing the willow twig, like a boy. Children were playing in the old graveyard next to the new, and Jepura would have liked to join them, and to tell the truth, so would I. Come spring, it takes great strength of character not to brandish a willow twig, or the stalk of a sunflower.

After three in the afternoon, an old woman shuffled out of the Jepura kitchen. I recognized her; she was Jepura's wife. She basked a little in the sun herself, and then sat down on the porch by Jepura's side. Except for when they bickered, they had not been this intimate in years, I think, and surely not since the previous spring. Carefully, I retreated from the window. God forbid I should disrupt any manner of courtship. Love, love of all kinds was made in heaven, even the spring-time love of an old married couple, and no man has the right to disturb it, or to turn his nose up at it.

Presently, wise old Jepura began to act like a young law student trying to impress some eminence at the local café. I could tell by certain signs that he had said some wickedly funny things, and he even took his wife's hands. He wooed her in his own way, just like thirty, thirty-five years before. The old woman giggled like a girl, and from time to time, slapped Jepura's hand. They did not notice that to the southwest, strange things were brewing in the sky. The clouds of the previous day had returned, dark and ugly, and proceeded to gulp down the sun. Old Mrs Jepura was just getting into the spirit of fun when it abruptly turned very dark. At this they both grew ashamed, especially Jepura, the wise. I had opened the window and was listening intently, for I wanted to hear as well as to see them by then. A chilling rain began to fall, and Jepura cursed, telling the old woman to go on inside.

"Aren't you ashamed, and old woman like you, acting like a school girl? With a man it's different, a man is different, a man can be foolish even if he's old. But you... how can you flirt, when Rachel Szelezsán is lying in her grave?"

The old woman snuck inside, while old Jepura and I gazed through the heavy rain in the direction of the graveyard, where just the day before they had taken the pretty, twenty-year-old Rachel Szelezsán who, perhaps, had never even known a kiss.

1908

Spring Mass

At the time of the spring floods, a woman came on a cart-and-four to Father Stephen, the priest of the Romanians. She was a Romanian farm woman herself, though well off and almost of the gentry, and her face was like the holy portraits of women found in country churches. The visit frightened Father Stephen, for he could still recall how at one time the compelling force of his youth and priesthood had rallied to produce mighty changes on the woman's pious countenance.

Now, however, the priest merely had to glance in a mirror and recall certain trials and tribulations that had since become his lot, and his mind was put at rest. Not even the spring floods could bring back the women of old any more, who were once many in number. The priest was sore afflicted in health, and it was with many a sigh and groan that he dragged himself out onto the portico and into the spring in order to greet his guest.

As she dismounted from her cart and approached him in the bright light of the sun, the priest stared.

She's just like she was five years ago, he thought, and felt disturbed in his shivering, miserable frame. In five years, Valéria hadn't even come to confession, though she used to be shriven every month. She went from her farmstead to other villages and other priests now, or into town, where she confessed and wept over her newly committed sins, for she was a sinful woman, though her face was like the St Annes of the primitives. She could look flirtatious even while chastising her soul with great repentances. Father Stephen, too, first transgressed with her, if only in thought, when she was making confession. This also happened during the time of the spring floods. Valéria knelt and, sobbing, beat her lovely brow against the confessional. Father Stephen could hardly calm her, and when he attempted to comfort her, saying that the Good Lord forgives even the greatest lechery, his words of solace were rewarded with a look of promise in Valéria's tear-drenched eyes.

Later, Valéria had her fill of Father Stephen and was terrified that she had sinned with the clergyman. She could feel the fires of hell scourching her body. She left the priest and, subdued in spirit and tearful, turned to another priest who absolved her, and who was well advanced in years. Ever since, Valéria would be shriven only by elderly priests, and would keep her eyes carefully lowered. In her simple soul, insatiable in sin yet perfect in piety, Valéria was St Anne left behind in the guise of a Romanian woman. The smell of incense always brought love to her mind, and love, the otherworldly mysteries.

The priest, who in the meantime had comforted himself once again with the thought that he was ill and God-fearing, went to greet Valéria.

"I thought you had forgotten me, Valéria, or else, that you were no longer among the living."

Valéria made no answer until she was in the priest's room, seated across from the crucifix hanging on the wall. Then she began to weep, a thing of beauty.

The priest set about to question her with some annoyance.

"I want a Mass," she wept, "say a Mass right away, regardless of expense."

"Is it for the dead, Valéria? Has someone close to you died? A relative perhaps?"

"He has not yet died but he will, as soon as Mass is said."

There was no one else in the house except for the maid servant softly singing somewhere nearby, in the kitchen, perhaps. The priest was a widower. The house was silent, and what slight noise there was came from the yard, where Valéria's coachman was curbing his unruly horses. The church was visible from one window, and the garden with its shimmering puddles from the other. Valéria, who sat facing the crucifix, glanced at Father Stephen now and then, but each time, she shuddered. What an image of death the strong, handsome man had become! And how silent!

At last, his mellow voice tainted with anger, Father Stephen spoke. He did not look at Valéria but at the garden window flooded with sunlight. For a moment, he tried to rest his eye on the window giving out unto the church, but he drew his glance away like a sinner, for close to his cheeks he felt his memories, he felt Valéria.

"Valéria, what you suggest is sacrilege. Mass is said only for the peace of the dead."

"He will be at peace, he must be at peace, once Mass is said for him. I cannot ask any other priest, but I can ask you, yes; you needn't know why you are saying it, all you need to know is that it was Valéria who asked you, whom you had kissed six years ago in church, before the Lord God, before His saints, and all His angels."

"Valéria," moaned Father Stephen, "what are you thinking? What is it you want?"

"My husband, he's a bad sort. He won't even attend church. I've grown weary of him. He bores me. I want him to pass away. I want him to die."

"We shall both be damned, may the Lord have mercy on our souls! Go! Go! I have one foot in the grave as it is!"

Valéria grabbed the priest's hand and, weeping, kissed it.

"I shall love you again as in the past, and the Lord shall forgive us. I shall go to the Bishop for confession, if you wish, and shall have a beautiful crucifix made for the road to Szatmár, a beautiful, gilded crucifix. And I shall have it fenced around, and have your name inscribed on it, as donor."

"No, no, Valéria. What you suggest is bad, I fear. It is terrible. Is your husband ill, and am I to say Mass for his recovery? Or for an easy death, if the Lord has so ordained?"

"He is not ill. But I want Mass said just the same, to ease his way."

*

Valéria planted another kiss on Father Stephen's hand. The priest shuddered and cursed himself, for he felt his physical ailments forsake him. The spring floods were sweeping him towards a deep, torrential river, and laughing, the sun bore down on his heart. He embraced Valéria, and his voice was tremulous as he spoke.

"I shall celebrate Mass tomorrow afternoon. But I do not wish to know what you have in mind. I shall say Mass so your wish may be granted, and so you may love me, Valéria."

"And I shall drive into town right away and bespeak the crucifix. It shall have your name carved on it, as the donor. It shall be beautiful. It shall be costly."

They kissed. Out in the yard, the coachman whipped his horses loudly, and Valéria shuddered. The maid servant was still singing, but the song seemed to come from a greater distance now. Then the coachman began to whistle a Romanian tune. But they did not hear him inside.

When she left, Mistress Valéria wept afresh, and crossed herself many times in front of the crucifix.

True to his word, the following day Father Stephen celebrated Mass. He felt sick and feverish. He took to his bed and for a forthnight thrashed about in the throes of a consuming fever. He was absolved by the priest of the neighbouring village and interred as a holy man, for it was on the self-same day that the crucifix bearing his name was set up on the road to Szatmár.

The day after the funeral, Valéria and her coachman, a fine-looking youth, murdered Valéria's husband, and buried him come nightfall. This was never discovered, and when Valéria visited the Bishop for confession, she said only that she had transgressed out of lechery. Ever since, Valéria has been even more devout, perhaps, than before, for deep down she is a god-fearing woman. Besides, Father Stephen had said Mass for the forgiveness of her sins – a spring Mass, said at the time of the spring floods.

1908

Flora

Flora's father, the mighty banker, bought Flora a husband. The deaf girl was past thirty, and becoming a greater tyrant of the house by the day, while her ears, her two truly shapely ears, God's own physician could have done nothing to cure.

Flora was almost twenty when adversity struck, a strange, sound-dampening affliction. They went from physician to physician, but nothing helped, neither medicine nor contrivance. Flora became deaf, and deaf as a post she remained; increasingly unbridled, too, she was, increasingly enamoured and homely. She even had to be kept from the man servants, and watched like an invalid.

The girl was highly strung, of oriental blood and fiery temperament. She was trouble. And how plain she was getting, year by year, day by day, how plain! She wallowed in self-torture and world-hatred, but enjoyed being happy, and was preparing some great revenge.

Meanwhile with her two younger sisters, lively and shapely of ear, she attended the Opera, where they had a box. She had adored music once, and sang, too, and now, night after night, watched in despair those bathed in music and sound. It was at the Opera that the gentleman her father had set his sights on was introduced to her. And with sagatious reasoning, this gentleman, the debonair Alexander, a kind of ne'er-do-well, took the bait.

After the wedding, Flora and Alexander did not go far for their honeymoon, and by nightfall had arrived at the elegant spa and hotel where their comfortable room was waiting for them. On the way, Alexander scribbled an entire notebook full of endearing nonsense. Yet it was mostly Flora who spoke, in the undertone of the deaf, rendered even more flat and subdued now by her passion. The deaf girl was enraptured, foolish, and excited, for her Alexander looked stalwart, acted chivalrous, and had the look of an opera hero.

Flora and Alexander kissed often on the way. But somehow, Alexander could not get himself to feel or believe of these kisses that they were kisses in earnest. He kissed Flora with lowered lids and the well-mannered routine of the experienced lover. A gentleman to the hilt, Alexander was the debonair darling of glamorous young ladies and women, and was accustomed, if need be, to sating himself without an appetite.

The newlyweds settled themselves in their rooms, ordered dinner, and drank champagne. Their windows looked out on the park. They moved to an open window and attempted to rob the summer night and moonlit garden of its atmosphere, to make it their own. For Flora this was easy, but Alexander was presently gripped by an unaccustomed, mortal fear. He was an ignoble man, and would have liked to laugh at this unreasonable fear. "She's not bad, really," he told himself; "besides, she's crazy about me."

And he may have been right. Love had made Flora almost beautiful, and the way in which she leaned her feverish head on Alexander's shoulder was almost enticing. But the fear and anxiety would not leave Alexander's side. He closed the casement and turned on all the lamps. He sat down in an easy chair and with a sigh, nervous and expectant, smoked a cigar.

In the meantime, Flora was in her room, changing into her negligée. She knew that she had lovely hair, and so unpinned it before going to her husband.

When Alexander saw Flora's hair, he felt a sudden surge of joy. This hair will be his deliverence, this hair will be his talisman, yes, this lovely hair! He hastened to bury his face in it, to see if it worked. The trial run was a success. Flora's hair was fragrant and silky; if one closed one's eyes, one could imagine a goddess, even, though Flora was a bony woman herself, whose freckled complexion had been distorted by single-minded effort at concentration, and whose body was in no wise that of a goddess. No, that could not be said for it.

She had stopped talking, and Alexander had ceased his scribbling. His small silver pencil had rolled off the table somewhere, he didn't care where.

The girl Flora, the would-be woman, cooed like a lovelorn adolescent. Alexander embraced her, kissing her brow and hair. Presently, his lips found one of the tiny, shapely, cold and deaf ears, and into this he whispered certain honeyed words of endearment. This banal point in his lovemaking schedule had always stood Alexander in good stead. But now he shuddered and blanched as if his lips had touched a corpse. He went in search of the other little ear to kiss. And then, superstition shook him to the core and benumbed him a hundredfold. His eyes began to play him false. He saw the two ears side by side, and they were not ears, but two monstrously deep, chilly graves, two graves attempting to gulp him down, to bury him for ever. He screamed. Flora did not hear. Then, raving, he sprang to his feet. Flora sprang up, too, and cried out when she saw him.

The debonair Alexander was frantically searching for his pencil. He wanted to communicate something to Flora. But the pencil had rolled away. Hunched over, with a rattle in his throat, Alexander plunged for it. It was gone. But he saw the huge mirror gleaming across the room. He ran over to it. He wore a magnificent diamond ring on his finger, a present from a woman of sweet memory. Like a lunatic, he scratched on the mirror, ten or twenty times, "I hate you!" Then he ran to the window, and in the other rooms as well he scratched on all the glass surfaces, "I hate you! I hate you!" And amidst Flora's deaf wails, he ran down the stars and was gone.

Summoned by a cable, the mighty banker arrived the following day. He smashed all the glass, and like a true gentleman, paid for the damage. Then, cursing, he dragged his deaf Flora, moaning and fainting all the while, back to her paternal home.

1907

The Mute Couple

Rudolf was a type-setter in a noisy printing shop which for him never made any noise at all. From sundown to sunup he turned stray letters into lead. And when the letters took the shape of words, they soared high up into the air. Rudolf could even see the wings of these airborne words. Sometimes in his delight, Rudolf would even yelp. He smacked his lips as if he meant to kiss the soaring words. For Rudolf was enamoured of words, words that he could see but not hear, for Rudolf was a deaf mute, a man incapable of speech.

When at dawn he reached home and lowered his scorching lids over his weary eyes, Rudolf would dream beautiful dreams. In his dreams he could speak. With hands clasped in the manner of the devout, he kissed the golden wings of the delicate word fairies. Attentive ears heard his speech and welcomed his winged messengers. Unfamiliar lips responded, and ever so gently, the words tickled Rudolf's ears. He could hear them. To him, they were like music.

Mistress Elizabeth of the cherry lips and tiny pink ears, who was Rudolf's wife, had dreams of a similar cast. But the words, the delicate yet heartless word fairies, she could not even see, though her eyes sparkled wide and azure into the world. Two little errant and unanchored souls, that's what they were. Then they found each other. They had drifted outside the bounds of the voluble world, and in this great, impenetrable silence, exchanged signs. They needed each other; they understood each other. With identically restless, abrupt gestures, they drew songs for each other in the air. And when in their fanciful souls, barred from life and vagrant in the world, they conjured up other lovers for themselves, deep down and in secret, lovers with hearing ears and singing lips beyond their comprehension, they huddled closer than ever and were grateful for another human being they could fathom.

They, the afflicted of speech, the banished, the orphaned, were once shaken by a long awaited joy. Rudolf almost made the printing shop tremble with his yelps. For those who understood his speech, with a profusion of gestures he explained, "A girl, a baby girl, a gorgeous baby girl! One day we will put her out to nurse. She will speak, like you, like everyone."

Months later, Rudolf was elated once again. He snapped his fingers. "I went like this next to her ear as she slept, and she heard. Tomorrow we are taking her away to nurse." And the adored, letter-engendered, inaccessible words fluttered past Rudolf's eyes on lovelier wings than ever, and he and Mistress Elizabeth dreamt more beautiful dreams, for their daughter, their very own daughter, was growing up. And they knew that she could speak. She was capable of speech. Her ears were kissed by sounds that were familiar to her, by words that escaped them, words incomprehensible, precious, divine. Now there would be someone to take them by the hand and guide them gently into the envied world of strangers with eloquent lips and hearing ears. For the time being, though, Elizabeth and Rudolf saw their daughter of the knowing lips and ears but seldom.

The child was growing up, and letters began to arrive. Never before such wonderful word fairies! They wouldn't leave Rudolf's side for a moment. Sometimes they shimmered as purple as the dawn. When Rudolf sweated in the printing shop, he would sometimes sneak one or another of these words into the unfamiliar lines of lead, while on the days that the letters came, in their tiny fourth storey flat, Mistress Elizabeth sang. Her immense joy stirred the slumbering reaches of her heart, and the song poured forth of its own accord. The wild, unmusical screeching disturbed the tenants, and when this happened, Mistress Elizabeth's big, azure eyes filled with tears.

Theirs was an immense and painful joy. Elizabeth and Rudolf could visit their daughter but seldom. Or else they would bring the child home, who, though far from frugal with her kisses, kissed them with trembling aversion. Frightened by their yelping speech, her eyes, even lovelier than Mistress Elizabeth's eyes, could barely catch the signs they made. Yet she was with them always, she who was the light of their errant souls, she, whose body was far removed, and to whom they had given the hearing ears and the lips of the sonorous, pearly words – they, the deaf and the speechless.

Then once it happened that Rudolf, who was getting on in years, and Mistress Elizabeth, whose countenance was wrinkled by now, did not see their daughter for a very long time. In order to further her education, kindly relatives had sent the girl to a distant town. Years later, though, she returned. A letter came for Mistress Elizabeth and Rudolf, a letter bringing wonderful news. Their daughter sang, she sang to the delight of all who heard her! For there is nothing more enchanting than someone singing. Oh, what joy it must be to hear someone sing!

Elizabeth and Rudolf set out for the town where their daughter had grown up. And on immense, impressive posters Rudolf read that the melodious child of their muteness would be singing that very night in a huge, brightly lit hall.

They settled themselves early in the brightly lit hall among the elegant, perfumed gentlefolk, and waited. Then they were overcome by a great numbness as they sat and attended wide-eyed to their daughter shimmering lambent before them in the gleaming radiance. They saw only the motion of her blood-red lips, they felt only the fevered excitement of the elegant folk. And they could see hands clap with admiration.

The sound, the sound... The song!... In front of Rudolf's eyes flittered a fiery legion of dazzling seraphim. Elizabeth's soul was stirred by a proud, dormant melody. Her enraptured spirit broke into song. She sent horrible yelping sounds towards her daughter. Rudolf broke into song, too. The people of the brightly lit hall turned into a frightened jumble. The police came and dragged the deaf ones away. They dragged them far away through pitch dark streets. And when they were released among the dark, unfamiliar houses in the night, the two deaf ones embraced. At that instant, their ears could hear. And they kissed each other with delirious joy, did Mistress Elizabeth and Rudolf.

1905

A Cleopatra Worth Ten Million

Cleopatra Gutberger had been living amid a flock of genteel young countesses for three years. In all of mightly, bustling Vienna, no one had a more exotic blondness than hers. Of all the German, Moravian and other types of contessas, her blood was surely the bluest, hers, Cleopatra Gutberger's, the sad little blonde child's, who was neither countess, nor contessa. This ever so exclusive, perfumed, fatuous boarding school – why, oh, why, did Cleopatra Gutberger have to attend it? Why couldn't Zsolt Gutberger of Nyír's ten millions rest in self-satisfied repose? No one knows; no one shall ever know. The secret to men's actions generally lies well concealed in the depths of time; every man's fate is contained in blood vessels long since turned to dust.

Zsolt Gutberger's ten millions rapped on the exclusive, perfumed palace door in Vienna, and Cleopatra soon called the German, Moravian, and other kinds of countesses by their first names. In turn, they loathed the charming, sad and exotic little blonde. This great loathing was fanned only by whispers, though, for the distinguished instructors and instructresses sided with Cleopatra. The ten millions were a gracious ten millions; Zsolt Gutberger of Nyír could afford to pay ten times, at least, for Cleopatra, what Prince Zedvitz-Hoch had laid out for his own freckled, coughing little princess.

Within this Viennese palace, rose-gardened and fenced about, Cleopatra appeared in the guise of the pale symbol of a new, shallow age. The escutcheoned scions of the robber barons sequestered themselves here in vain; everywhere, the commoner millions followed in their wake. With the siege of his ten millions, for instance, Zsolt Gutberger could march his own brood in anywhere he liked. This is what Cleopatra stood for.

The genteel little countesses were wont to whisper all sorts of things. With a shudder, one gave vent to the suspicion that Cleopatra's grandfather had been a Jew, while a Croatian baronness with mixed blood and a strange name fancied that the Gutbergers had been Hungarian cattle dealers.

"No, no!" protested the daughter of a shabby-genteel Hungarian count and army officer who was there through the agency of well-placed friends, "I've heard of the Gutbergers. They were Israelites once, but Cleopatra's mother was born a Roman Catholic, the daughter of an indigent man of letters, now dead."

"But how could such riffraff be so wealthy?" screeched Fraulein Zedvitz-Hoch.

How indeed? Night after night, his own millions

asked Zsolt Gutberger of Nyír the same question. "For it could not be otherwise," must have been what widowed Zsolt Guberger of Nyír answered with the sweat of his brow. But the big bank notes said nothing. At times they may have radiated a blood-red light, the resurrected heart's blood of foolish, ne'er-do-well, impassioned, brilliant men; their renewed life's blood came bursting forth from the bank notes.

These good-for-nothing fellows composed music once, wrote plays, poetry and novels; they carved statues and dabbled with paint. And mostly, they perished on the ragged edge so that the Gutberger fortune could multiply. And multiply it did. Like a vampire did this fortune fling itself at the artists' hearts. But it could bring sacrifices for this bloody fare as well. Zsolt Gutberger of Nyír married Cleopatra's mother because Cleopatra's grandfather had written voluminous novels. He nearly starved to death in the process, but there was little doubt that some day these novels would be sought after, and might even make a fortune – provided they fell into the right hands. And so, Zsolt Gutberger took Cleopatra's mother to be his lawfuly wedded wife.

Sure enough, the novels brought in the hundreds of thousands. Then, having presented two boys and a girl to the Gutberger millions, from the combined effects of early consumption and a sacred sense of duty, Cleopatra's mother passed away, though not before she could transfer the heart's blood of her brilliant, ne'er-do-well novelist father from her own into the Gutberger blood vessels.

71

Ever since, the ghost of this woman of early consumption haunted Zsolt Gutberger of Nyír, who proved powerless against it. After many a detrimental though sweet scandal, many a solem paternal curse, one of his sons, the cavalry officer, joined the Foreign Legion and fell somewhere in Africa. The other son suffered a far worse fate. With his poems and articles he had to go begging from newspaper to newspaper, and was elated if he could come into the sacred presence of some crude, dishevelled scribe. Zsolt Gutberger of Nyír mourned the cavalry officer, but of the ways of the dissolute son still living he refused so much as hear. He had no one left just Cleopatra, who at the time of our story had been living in Vienna for three years among the genteel little countesses, and who was the promise of a coronet that was seven pointed, and to which the Gutberger millions had earned the right.

"Away with you, pale female shadow! You had given birth to abominable sons while you were the wife of Zsolt Gutberger of Nyír. But over your daughter you shall have no sway. She shall become a baronness, or the wife of a prince at the very least," thought Zsolt Gutberger. "She is a clever, haughty, and excellent creature, a true Gutberger. She surely looks down her nose at all her shoolmates, too. How inconsequential it is to be born a baronness! How much more potent and promising it is when someone is called Cleopatra Gutberger of the Ten Millions!"

Just stay sequestered for some time yet in Vienna, among the genteel little countesses, Cleopatra Gutberger, haughtier than any of them. Despite a paltry female shade, this is how Zsolt Gutberger will have it. It is how he will have it. You needn't even bother to come home till then. Costly school mistresses shall show you Paris, Rome, and the miraculous lights of the North. Just write no more diaries!

The diary in question had been discovered under Cleopatra's pillow, and an anxious letter was soon dispatched to Zsolt Gutberger of Nyír. "The child is highly strung, by disposition introspective, fanciful, a dreamer." But that was now in the past. A year had gone by since, with no cause for alarm. Youngest of the whole fragrant flock, Cleopatra proved to be a princess among the magnates' daughters. She was not yet sixteen, and yet was the most mature by far, and the brightest as well. She was even familiar with the stories of all the paintings in the Belvedere. She gave the best answers in history, excelled in physics, played the piano and the violin. Cleopatra was perfect, just that she had grown cold as ice of late. She didn't have a single friend. She was haughty and aloof, too, said the latest dispatches about Cleopatra, and this pleased Zsolt Gutberger of Nyír. Just so. Let the girl mend the harm her brothers had caused. Let Cleopatra the haughty ward off the paltry female shade that had been her mother ere she turned to shade!

Then the three years that in the exclusive Viennese

palace saw Cleopatra grow more and more wonder-
fully blonde were drawing to a close, and a bustling
spring came to meet them. The fragrant young ladies
were habitually taken for strolls to fragrant Viennese
parks, and even the Pater, now and then. It was here,
perhaps, that with their cute little noses up in the
air, smiling and making funny faces, the fragrant
young ladies first saw the Italian vagabond wearing
loose fitting, dirty clothes and a cloak of velvety
memory. The tattered vagabond was trying to force
blooming trees and sunlight onto his canvas. It was
a desperate effort. The idle fellow had a torpid heart
instead of a dreamy one, ambitions, but without
energy to match. His ruddy face, bright eyes, small
moustache, the locks of black matted hair falling
over his brow – his entire exotic and grubby aspect,
in fact, made the vagabond as fascinating as the
devil.

After this stroll, the genteel young ladies talked
about him for days. They made fun of him. They
teased each other because of him. Then as luck
would have it, the strolling girls saw the Italian
again in another place. They had wandered into a
suburban alley, where the painter was standing by
the window of a low cottage, still trying his hand at
the blooming trees and the sunlight. His expression
was pained. When he saw the girls he was vexed
and gave his battered easel a kick. He was in shirt
sleeves and whistled as he followed the closely
chaperoned flock with his eye. Mischievously and in
secret, some of the litte countesses waved to him.

Flanked by two grave school mistresses, Cleopatra marched in the back, haughy and proud as any queen.

At this time of the year, the windows of the girls' sleeping quarters were left open. The end of May had come, and out in the garden bloomed many fragrant flowers. The night was moonlit, the time eleven, and the silence profound. In the dark, Cleopatra slipped out of bed and into her clothes. From under her mattress she drew the things she had stolen and hidden there – a candle, matches, and a notebook she called her diary – and with suppressed sobs, burnt the tattered bundle. The late-spring night poured its intoxicating perfume through the window. Cleopatra slept alone on the ground floor. She jumped out the window. It was just nine feet, a mere nothing. The high garden wall of stone bruised her hand, but she climed over it just the same. Then she broke into a run...

Zsolt Gutberger of Nyír must have waged his mightiest battle with the pale female shade on that night. On that night, Zsolt Gutberger must have dreamt terrible dreams. He might have even screamed in his sleep. For it was at that hour that in an alley outside a cottage, in the late-May night, Cleopatra Gutberger of Nyír sobbed and beat a window with her fists until, with an intoxicating laugh and eager arms, she was swept up by the very bad Italian painter to be whisked inside his miserable, one-bedded hovel to join him beside his canvas of badly painted trees in bloom and soulless bit of sunshine.

1904

Olga and the Blonde Danube

Olga set out on her uncertain journey near Vienna. "No, no! No use looking at me like that. I don't want you any more!" A tattered painter had said this to her somewhere on the outskirts, and cruelly. And so, Olga set out.

She was not a smart girl, but she was proud. Though it was night, she refused to go back home – or at least, that's what she thought. And that it had been night, too, when she had ran away from the most fragrant of girls' rooms for the sake of the tattered one.

She dragged her lovely young body along with an effort, but she reached the Danube at last. She knew that she could do it. Trembling took no hold of her, though the night breeze nipped her skin, for it was March. Splash! Let's go! The setting out was ugly, but shortlived. A new and more merciful tide came and received Olga upon its gentle lap, and the journey began.

There seemed to be no riverbank anywhere, ever. Water vehicles of all sizes seemed to go around her.

The paddles of the water mills sang to her from a safe distance. The Danube carried her lovely body, newly cleansed into maidenhood, with something like pride and affection. And wherever Olga went, at some ways from the riverbank, life continued on its humming way. People scampered about in pursuit of their meagre ambitions. There were tattered ones among them, too. And no one suspected that hidden in the deep blondness of the river, someone was approaching from Vienna, not knowing how much longer she'd have to go, or where she'd end up, all because of a tattered youth.

"See, Gyuri Szabó, this is your life. You're back again, living off the river, like a frog." Thus did Gyuri Szabó address Gyuri Szabó. He was standing moodily on the Danube's bank, pronouncing his words in the strange manner of the people of Csallóköz. He worked with net and trap, cursing as he did so, but softly, for the village lay close by, and he might be overheard.

It was a sweet, pristine spring morning. Gyuri Szabó cast his net, glanced about, and muttered to himself. He was a young man. He was just thirty. He was a simple man with nerves of steel, living a life of hardship, one of the poor folk of the land in whose loveliest love songs, even, there lies ensconced the yearning, oh, how nice it would be to eat meat every day! And because he had his hands full with the time and the river, he was discontented and crafty. He loathed the water and the fish. He felt that the girls, too, were reluctant to kiss him only because he didn't live off the land. A frog, a repulsive frog, that's what he was. And then, he glanced in the direction of the village.

He first took account of the better houses. He was angry, and in his anger, repeatedly shook his head. But then he'd forget about his head, and stare stiffly somewhere at the upper end of the village. Whenever he caught himself doing it, he was furious.

"What's the use of looking? She isn't there. She's up in Pest, strolling down fancy roads in fancy dresses. Fine. Who cares. She wouldn't have a pauper, that's clear. She hankered for a gentleman, not a peasant. Well, that's just fine with me!"

And he cursed. Though he said it was fine, it hurt around his heart, or whatever. And he imagined how a girl called Zsuzsika who'd have nothing but Pest had been living now for five days in that far off city of fancy mansions.

Gyuri Szabó felt that a girl who had no peer in all of Csallóköz must be at least as indulged in Budapest. She wanted to go into service; only, she'll never be a servant, not that one! Five days! By now she must be like a countess. She must have a sweetheart too, by now, a fine gentleman in patent leather shoes. Zsuzsika wouldn't want Gyuri Szabó any more.

At this, a strange, muddled feeling came over Gyuri. He'd been to town often enough. And there were gentlemen aplenty living in the village as well. He reflected that the trouble was, somehow, that there were gentlemen in the world at all. Gentlemen, they're like peacocks. They never worry themselves with nets. They never work as hired hands. They eat, drink, smoke paper cigars, and kiss. And the girls, especially the girls, they hide their delicate complexions behind veils. They wear fine bodices and feathered hats so they practically flutter. And even if they don't so much as look at a man, they're so provocative, a man's all distracted. Gyuri remembered how often he'd watched them. Well, Zsuzsika wanted to be like that too, he reflected. A gentleman-fetching, veiled and silk-stockinged lady. In his fury, he felt like running at the Danube.

"So you want to be a lady, do you? Fine with me. Just fine with me. Fine with me!" He must have said "fine with me" ten times, at least, though he knew that it was not fine at all.

"If only I could lay my hands on a lady like that, I'd strangle her right this minute, yes I would! But their kind don't come to these parts. Why should they? They're up in the city, because that's where the gentlemen are. They have their fun up there, while you, Gyuri Szabó, pick at the water like a toad."

Meanwhile, the Danube carried Olga on her merry way. But all at once, the voyager stopped. The dead girl, the lovely and insensate voyager, may have been surprised, even, if indeed the dead are ever surprised on their beautiful voyages at all. Why don't they let her go on her way? On her way?...

Gyuri Szabó took a good look at his net. An ugly word escaped his lips, a coarse word. Is this why he'd been toiling? A woman! No fish, just a dame.

The devil had it in for him again. If his anger hadn't been tempered by a bit of curiosity, he'd have flung the body right back, then and there. But he's got to be on his guard, he knew. The village is a stone's throw away. He could easily get into trouble. It would be a bad enough business if the village had to bury the body. They'd be all over him because of the expense. But if the magistrate should find out, he'd be in trouble for failing to report it. And somehow, even the brutal and beastly notion came to him that man is nothing but trouble to his fellows, even when he – or she – happens to be dead. Then he gave the body a closer look.

He coughed nervously. "Gentlefolk, of course. A lady. So what have we been up to Miss? Have we grown sick of all those nice oranges and cakes? Is that it? Or have we cheated on one gentleman after another? What a nun's face the wench has got! And eyes as pious as Zsuzsa's."

Talking all the while, he was handling the body more roughly now. "Naturally, you were pleased to leave your valuables behind. This small ring? It's not much. And the fancy comb? The little miss had lovely hair. And these shoes. What use are they? They're yellow, and hardly fit for a four-year-old."

As he worked, Gyuri Szabó cast guarded glances in the direction of the village. "What if they should recognize the ring and the comb?" he remembered. That would mean severe punishment. He pulled it back on the stiff little finger of the left hand. The comb he hid inside the black stresses, swollen, wet,

81

yet lovely. But now an even greater fury raged within his crafty, discontented soul. He'd been working in vain, he thought. He'd caught no fish. Zsuzsika was up in Pest with her gentlemen. She'd become a lady. A lady! Gyuri Szabó raised his hand and struck the lovely face, so peaceful and pale. Then he gave the dead girl such a shove that the water splashed all over his face.

"Go on your way, Missy, go! Go on down Zsuzsi's path!"

And resuming her voyage in the blonde depths of the humming river, Olga continued on her way.

1905

Post Mortem

You'd think Turgenyev had breathed life into her once, and now she meant to fade, like a dream, a Russian story, white and sad, a tattered, anaemic Russian poem... Her name was Sonya, but she might just as easily have been called Tatiana, for she was as thoroughly Russian as only a Jewish girl can be. She had come with her mother, uncle, and five little brothers and sisters from around Odessa, or so she said. She said she had seen her father killed, it happened on a Friday night, they were at their evening prayers when the house caught fire above their heads.

And surely this is just how it must have happened, for why would Sonya have lied about these things? Where else could her eyes have learned their wild bewilderment? For there was great bewilderment in Sonya's eyes, the bewilderment of red roosters and of murderers, the bewilderment of flight. Her uncle, a tall, burly, gruff and ugly Jew, did not call her Sonya, but Tzirle. It is an ancient Jewish name, they say, and it is lovely, Tzirle, Tzirle, as if plucked off the strings of a harp.

In short, they found themselves in Paris, where Sonya gained entry to the homes of her betters to mend their cheap clothes. She spoke only Russian and that dreadful language of Slavic Jews of which only the Moorish-Latin speech of Malta is more hateful to the ear.

But Sonya learned French quickly, for she had read Tacitus and was familiar with the Greek poets. She had finished grammar school, and in anticipation of her future prospects, the people of the small town from where she hailed had already addressed her as Miss Lady Doctor. Indeed, she might have been a doctor by now, had not the governor back home passed a law: Jewish girls could leave their homes for the big city only if they were willing to become ladies of the night. So Sonya decided to wait. Then that dreadful Friday night came, and they fled. Sonya, however, could not forget her father. When drunken peasants shouted through the window, Sonya's father went outside to investigate. She heard his cries for help, and the thatched roof went up in flames. The family ran outside, and she saw her father by the bright light, lying in the middle of the yard, his head split in two. His eyes, though, were intact.

Sonya, or Tzirle, continued to see her father's eyes even in Paris – his angry, pained, glaring eyes. And she earned money for her mother, who was blind, and for her brothers and sisters. She even put a little aside. She studied French diligently and was looking forward to the day when she would have enough money to become Miss Lady Doctor in earnest.

She was soon past twenty-four, and the angularity of her body took on a more pleasing shape. She learned to take care of herself, her whiteness and hereditary delicacy, both hidden and manifest. She learned to dress, to hold her skirts, to walk with a provocative gait. She even learned to smile. Only her eyes would learn nothing to replace the long-ingrained image of that Friday night.

It was not easy, indeed, to look into those eyes, for Sonya shielded them well. Only when she was mending the cheap clothes, threading her needle or following its course with her eyes could one steal a glance, perhaps, and even then only to suspect that those eyes of living memory were big, brown, profound, exceptional, restless, yet cold.

At last, Sonya had put sufficient money aside to enroll at the university and study to her heart's content. She met a Russian student, the type of Russian whose posturings were reminiscent of the romantic Poles of the early nineteenth century. He was a handsome youth prone to melancholy, who castigated oppression with full, intense lips. He received a liberal monthly stipend from his father, a provincial commissioner and country squire back home. He was a medical student, too, but Russian, with proud, unbounded dreams, despotic inclinations, and barbaric strength. And Sonya's eyes began to change. They turned sky-blue and sparkled with the fire of hitherto unfamiliar suffering. The Russian youth was a handsome youth, and his voice, which never failed to bring a blush to the cheeks of the most retiring of women, oh! his voice was ever so enchanting!

Sonya, or Tzirle, no longer even dared think about who she was or what had happened to her. Sometimes in the night she would beat her brow in despair, and her head and her lips, which longed to kiss, yes, and she remembered the young, noble Russian clerks back home with the good connections. She remembered, too, the village squires who used to visit her small town on carriages drawn by black Crimean horses. They were just like her Russian, except they did not preach revolution and did not go to Paris to study medicine. But in that case, what did this youth want from Sonya, no, not Sonya, but Tzirle?

Once Sonya was in medical school and was no longer mending cheap clothes, there was much trouble at home. One of her little brothers made a bit of money, and with her blind eyes Sonya's mother took in wash, work she did in great earnest. One of Sonya's ten-year-old sisters kept an eye on the clothes in the tub and told her mother when they needed more scrubbing. Sonya's uncle, the tall, gruff and burly Jew, would still visit them on occasion, but Paris had so refined him that now he handed out advice only, but financial assistance never. And he rebuked Sonya for her ambition.

It happened during the first post mortem. Sonya awaited this great occasion with dread. They brought a reddish-blonde man from the morgue. He had been fished out of the Seine and kept on ice for some time, for there was an investigation into his affairs: his head had been split in two. But as nothing came to light, the corpse was handed over for the benefit of the students, the doctors of the future.

The dead man was a tall, blonde youth, a tough, Semitic type. He was lying on the table, the professor was lecturing, and an assistant and two aids were bustling about. Sonya and perhaps thirty others, all young, three or four women among them, stood around the dissecting table. Suddenly, Sonya found her former eyes with their former bewilderment. Oh, just like her father! The eyes are intact in the head! And how angry they are. They are looking right at her, too, at Sonya and the Russian, of whom Sonya used to dream.

The professor called on the Russian first, who approached the corpse with a knife. That instant a strange, atavistic rage took hold of Sonya. As she watched how coolly the Russian was approaching the split-headed corpse, the blood rushed to her head, and she pounced on him, whom she so dearly loved.

"Murderer! Son of murderers! How many times would you kill a man?"

The students and aids could hardly restrain the poor girl who, now somewhat advanced in years, is once more mending cheap clothes at the homes of her better.

1908

Neighbours of the Night

This Menton* here is a hateful place. As I had a slight fever the other day, I spent the time thinking. I know perfectly well that I have just two more weeks to live. These big, blue mountains will drive me into the sea. I shall die here, no doubt. What was the use of sending me here? I gasp for air in vain with my tubercular lungs. I stroll along the promenade, gazing out to sea. And I wait for the approach of death.

Life has played a nasty trick on me. As if I did not have enough troubles of my own to contend with! Life is a bloody, feverish, deathly affair at best. And now, every moment, that Other comes to mind.

Who is that Other, you ask? Once a fine but penniless blonde called him Ottóka. So the other is called Ottó. How is he faring, I wonder? Where is he now, the Ottó I do not know? By the Nile? Or wasting away in Budapest? Has he been taken to the Tátra**

* An elegant health resort on the French Riviera.

** The mountain range in Slovakia, then still part of Northern Hungary, where there were also several popular health resorts.

to breathe crisp mountain air? Or is he in Switzerland, perhaps?

I miss this Ottó. I often weep on account if him. I am afraid that this Ottó will die just as I shall die. And who shall take our places then back in Budapest? Will only men with healthy lungs and healthy ambitions board the street-cars once we are gone?

I am furious with this Ottó. He should realize the impropriety of dying. He is nothing but a miserable painter. What does a painter want from life? He should have been content to paint. He should have been content to have a woman look at him every now and then. But no! He is dying instead. Well, he has no right! I am very annoyed with him. Life has given me a rough turn. I had my share of sorrow. I have a right to die. But Ottó has no right at all... And now, I think I should tell you our story.

Summer was fading in Budapest back then, and a grey, chilly autumn had descended on the region of the Danube. Mighty disappointments drove me into the night. Every part of the twenty-four hours is terrifying, but in Budapest, the most terrifying is the day. People tread on each other's heels. Pain and doubt sit on every face. Every man alive is your enemy. The life of daytime Budapest is one huge, protracted groan. And so, I turned for solace to the night.

What was I doing in the night? I want young ladies to read this story of mine. So I shall only say that I led an unseemly, dissolute life. But rose clouds of ecstasy floated densely above my head, while women laughed brightly into my mournful thoughts. The fervour of mighty moments engulfed my soul. If my lungs were up to it, I would go right back into the night. It made me feel thoroughly masculine often enough to satisfy me. And is this not the be-all and end-all of life? A crying shame that the lung is such a weak machine.

I always woke at dusk. I dressed by lamplight. My head felt hot, my eyes vacuous. Nighttime Budapest was making its habitual noises, and I set out in anticipation.

And every time I boarded the street-car, Ottó boarded as well. He was his usual weary self. Then once he was engaged in conversation with someone. It was then that I learned that Ottó paints. He comes to this part of town at dawn, to work in his studio. He works till dusk, then heads back home. He reads a little, then sleeps through the night.

I was annoyed with him the instant I saw him. I had thoughts like: This man is no older than I. Probably, he is also daring enough to have dreams. He is absorbed in the study of life. He would like to have it all to himself, just like me. And he must curse a great deal, too. But he is just a miserable painter, all the same. So why doesn't the bastard paint? What good is thinking to a man like him? Why does he bother? What does he want from life? These bunglers just burden our own destinies. Few men have the right to crave or curse life. And this Ottó is not one of them. After all, he lives by day. For him, dawn brings the imperative to work. This Ottó is just a regular drudge.

Neighbours of the night, that's what we were. We eyed each other with anger and distrust. Our neighbourliness was most curious. I set out to live the life of the day, a life that lay dormant, waiting for me in the night; Ottó had already lived through the day and was heading home to rest. Our mutual encounter fell at six o'clock in the evening. Almost every night we boarded the same street-car. Our eyes were equally round, our shaven faces flaccid and yellow.

Ottó's expression pained and haunted me. I fell to thinking. This man lives by the day. I should ask him, for I have long since forgotten: are things more matter-of-fact by day? Are people less foolish? Is there a different flavour to a daytime kiss? Are one's sinews stronger? Is the clickity-clack in our brains less severe? Do we hope to get more out of life?

Every evening, Ottó gazed sadly and contemptuously into these thoughts of mine, as if laughing at them through his tears. I would get nothing out of him, I felt.

Once Ottó got on the street-car with a woman, the same penniless blonde who had called him Ottóka. She treated him like a dog. He whimpered. And this satisfied me enormously. (See, you miserable daytimer? Women are no better at your time of the day!) And during the night that followed, I was in exceedingly high spirits.

Another time on the street-car, Ottó was deep in conversation with a big-bellied gentleman. The big-bellied gentleman was himself a painter, but a clever one. He was a very well-to-do gentleman. He slapped Ottó on the back repeatedly, and called him a foolish young man. ("Never mind, never mind. There will always be foolish young men, I see. It was the same in my day, and it is as it should be. Youthfulness is foolishness. Let the young feel that the world expects great things from them. Well, it expects a great big nothing, that is what it expects! I would have starved to death years ago had I not purged my thoughts of such nonsense. It is not brush and canvas you want, young man, but life. And friends. You want to wrap people around your little finger.")

Poor Ottó. He wore his heart on his sleeve. I would have liked to pounce on the big-bellied gentleman, to scream and bite his belly. But the devil got the better of me, and I felt ecstatic instead. (See, Ottó? You live by the day. You live the reverse of the life I live. And what do you get out of it, Ottó? Well? Are you any stronger, Ottó? Ottó, Ottó, I shall see you in the night yet!)

The big-bellied gentleman got off the street-car. Ottó's expression was pained. He looked at me. He must have felt what I felt.

Winter came, and Budapest was more suffocating than ever. I was past my initial shock by then. When first I spotted the blood on my handkerchief, I groaned. But one gets used to it. In just two weeks, I came to accept the approach of death with glee.

Ottó was punctual, and so was I. On these evenings, he was pale and unusually withered. He sat across from me and was seized by a fit of coughing. I looked and saw the blood on his lips. (Bravo, Ottó! Though, really, it is rather impudent of you, imitating me like this. We are banal chaps, you and I. We could have avoided destroying our lungs like this, you know. But you are scared of the revolver, Ottó, and so am I.) Ottó's big, round eyes glistened. They were just like mine. (So death lies in ambush during the day, too, old chap? Couldn't your way of life save you, either? That is not much consolation to those who regard life as something worth writing home about. You will die, Ottó, and you haven't even compared the night with the day.)

This is how it happened, and I have not seen my neighbour since. I am awaiting death here, in this hateful Menton. But Ottó, where is Ottó, I wonder? I am furious with this chap. He should have taken better care of himself. With me, it is different. I am of no consequence.

1906

A Hundred-Thousand Forints

I.

Having lived a good and generous life, once there died in Cairo a wealthy Hungarian gentleman. But though still in his prime at the time of his death, he had left behind a testament, and in this testament he bequeathed the engineer Tamás Kovács a hundred-thousand forints. The deceased gentleman from Cairo had such a fabulous fortune that for him a hundred-thousand forints were as one. But for Tamás Kovács, the hundred-thousand forints seemed greater than all the treasure of Darius, and the way it came, too, was like a bolt from the blue. For Tamás Kovács had not seen as much as one thousand forints together in all his life. And the gentleman, too, who had died in Cairo he'd seen just once, and even then, at a distance.

This gentleman had a mansion in the small town where Tamás Kovács lived a life of hardship. From time to time he would come home, give dinners, or attend balls. Tamás Kovács had no liking for illustrious gentlemen, and so avoided making his acquaintance. But Mrs. Kovács was less fortunate.

She encountered the owner of the mansion a few times, once at a tea party given by the wife of the county judge, and once at a concert, where her husband was unable to accompany her. And yet, for no apparent reason, from his deathbed, this illustrious gentleman had flung a hundred-thousand forints at the Kovács family.

When first he heard the news, Tamás Kovács thought that he must be the victim of a practical joke. Then he felt as though the law were banging his door, accusing him of murder. The small town laughed behind his back and bristled with envy, but even the most died-in-the-wool detractors could come up with nothing definite.

After a while, Tamás Kovács locked himself up with his wife in order to settle accounts.

"I demand to know what that infamous womaniser meant by leaving you all that money!"

Mrs. Kovács did not appear offended, nor was she surprised or scandalised.

"Tamás, you cannot be in earnest! How should I know that any better than yourself?"

"I shall turn that money down right now, right this minute!"

"Do as you see fit, Sir! You know about such matters better than I!"

For several days yet, Tamás Kovács continued indignant and thunderstruck. But all along, the hundred-thousand forints were weaving their spell and bedazzling him, even in his dreams. So in the end, Tamás Kovács decided to accept the preposterous, but handsome sum.

II.

Mrs. Kovács was not in love with her husband when she married him, but she was not in love with anyone else either, for that matter, before or since. She was the kind of striking beauty who put the local gentlemen on their guard. She was a woman without a plan, besides – sluggish of blood, of curiosity limited, of sensuality that was almost nill. When a young man's blood would stir in her presence, she would notice, no doubt, but she was not scandalised. Nor did she put up her defenses, for she was in no danger. No one knew this better than the gentleman who had died in Cairo. Though who can say? This is all speculation and conjecture, while women, too, are only human. One thing alone is certain: the gentleman who had died in Cairo is no longer in a position to tell us.

In the wake of the hundred-thousand forints, Tamás Kovács experienced all the pains for which, truth to tell, he was little destined, and for which he had precious little talent. Even if he could have come to terms with himself and make his peace, there was the world to be reckoned with. And the world, especially the small corner of it in which they lived, would not forgive the hundred-thousand forints. No matter. The Kovácses moved to another town. The news, however, followed in the wake of the money, and its curse weighed like lead on Tamás Kovács's soul. A thousand times did he swear that he'd squander away the damnable, wretched sum.

But alas, poor Tamás Kovács had no talent for that either.

If anything, Mrs. Kovács suffered even more unjustly. Her husband treated her like a corrupt creature who must be locked away from the plainest of men. "Surely, you have sold yourself," was the accusation he levelled at her whenever one of his wild moods took the better of him.

And the lovely Mrs. Kovács began to lose her looks with alarming rapidity. But because her husband's accusations stood as constant reminder of her beauty, her instincts were aroused. More than once would she tell her husband defiantly, "You should be proud, Sir, that your wife's kisses are held in such high esteem. Who knows? I may have deserved even more than the hundred-thousand forints!"

III.

Tamás Kovács and his wife led their lives of torment in a manner ugly to behold. And as they advanced in years, more and more each saw the other as the baneful ruin of life. They were haunted by the hundred-thousand forints and their secret. The inate common sense of their class curbed them for a while. But one day they were forced to admit that they had grown old. To Tamás Kovács it occurred that he had been made to lead a simple, decent life indecently, while Mrs. Kovács's nights were disturbed by the thought of all the unjust accusations hurled at her head. Her husband kept her jealously guarded under lock and key, he abused her and destroyed her celebrated good looks.

Mrs. Kovács had already withered and Tamás Kovács had grown bald when the curse took its final stranglehold on them. They had no children who with their innocent, questioning eyes could have protected and restrained them. And so, old and raging, they set out on the road on which the liberal minded gentleman of Cairo had ended his own days. Tamás Kovács, the miserly Tamás Kovács, began to squander his money on women, like chaff. Mrs. Kovács put on airs, gave dinners, travelled, and by force, if need be, would settle for nothing less than the attentions of young men.

It was like an avalanche made inevitable by a loosened rock. One man alone hovered over the fates of this wild couple – the wealthy gentleman who had died in Cairo, and of whom only Mrs. Kovács could have said anything to herself for certain.

Torn by ignominy, destitute and cursing, Tamás Kovács and his wife died in quick, fortunate succession as only the innocent know how. It is my contention, though I may be mistaken, that with this bit of capricious revenge, the deceased gentleman from Cairo had meant to avenge himself for a night of love that had once been denied him.

1908

Death's Little Coach-and-Four

Death's sad and pale faced coachman was a Hungarian lad. Death had hired him, but put no horses under his care. Death just seared his skull-and-bones insignia on his coachman's brow; let those who wish to see this terrible sign do so. For the time being, though, Death's Coachman used his cracking whip to lash out at the empty air.

Once it transpired that Death's Coachman set out for Budapest. He felt that his master would be needing him soon, and he wished to see one last time the places where he had been Life's humble servant.

Death's Coachman had a long way to go. Many places were beckoning to him, many places claimed him. The flowery past sent its most intoxicating perfumes his way. Death's Coachman brandished his whip. The grand, airy strength of the Great Plain drew his sickly body like a magnet. He forgot Budapest utterly, and the nights when he had been consumed by fever.

But snow clouds gathered overhead, and soon winter

made its appearance. When Death's Coachman had set out from Budapest, spring had laughed its endearment, but by the time he reached his tiny native village, the winter squall was howling in earnest.

"How shall I come upon the traces of the former women here?" signed Death's Coachman. He was a male, after all, and the male is engaged in the perpetual pursuit of the female. If he loves life and is betrothed to the future, he will no doubt go to meet women newly approaching and as yet unfamiliar. But if broken in spirit, he must face his past, and will certainly go to look for the women of old. Women, after all, were created to stand as signposts on the highway of men's lives.

Death's Coachman went in search of the first trace to a farmyard overgrown with rosemary, where love had first bloomed for him. He was not yet five then, perhaps, but some men are born neurasthenic and taste of love's disappointment at a tender age.

The yard overgrown with rosemary was now slumbering beneath the snow with no trace of little Julie anywhere, little Julie, with whom Death's Coachman had once hidden there in order to steal a kiss. Even memories seemed to flutter in this yard gently, as if from behind a snowy mantle. White and cold, winter had covered little Julie's traces with windswept snow. Nor was there a sign of Elizabeth anywhere, who had been a little peasant girl. And felled was the poplar under which Death's Coachman used to play with the Jewish Gisella.

"Where are the girls, the girls of yesteryear? Shall I ever see the traces of their dainty feet? The Romanian Flora, the servant girl Margie, the genteel, vacationing Dora, the French bonne, the German Luiza, the priest's daughter, where are they now? Has Life taken them by the arm to lead them down silken paths like a gentleman? Where are the former girls today?"

Death's Coachman sighed once more and felt the urge to return to Budapest. But he resumed his journey just the same. There is no getting around women, not even once they are gone. Death's Coachman cracked his whip. Gidde-up, you disembodied horses, in the wake of the women who have fled! But there was snow and frost everywhere. The village gave way to small towns. Here, too, there had been girls once who had exchanged merry words and daring kisses with Death's Coachman. By now he had to subdue his tears whenever he thought of Budapest, where there was light and steam, at least, and where the girls came to laugh merrily into one's ears of their own accord. But he craved the former women, the women that were real. They had all gotten up and fled from Death's Coachman, it seemed. Rosette had been the kindest, for at least, she had sent him her husband.

"Rosette, who was my wife? She left us five years ago. She bore me a son, then moved down to the graveyard."

("The first sign in the snow: a gravemound and a mischievous, badly washed boy. Rosette, Rosette, so you were the most faithful to me after all. You, at least, have sent word about what Life had given you, and how it had treated you.")

But the rest remained silent. Irma and her husband had run away from the small town one night. Of Theresa, no one had any news. Death's Coachman felt a profound sadness settle in his soul. Could he have brought death to all those he had once approached? Of Ilka he learned that she was a widow, and wasting away in bed on account of her bad lungs. Ugh, how horrible! He shall get her out of his thoughts. But who else was there of the former girls?

By then he was in a place where women had first inflamed his youthful heart. But a woman is never of the past, and seldom of the future; a woman is always of the present. A woman is the girl who is no more. But Death's Coachman wandered around the pathways of the past, and would have nothing but the girls of yesteryear. He wished to see whether these girls had given anything to Life and to the future.

Reluctant and apprehensive, he left Blanka, the girl among girls, for last. His manhood was first stirred into life when he had met her. The girl among girls is the one of whom we dream so hard in our tender youth that blushing, we must knock on the doors of grave, disapproving physicians. It is these girls who bring the man out of us and present Life with all its splendour on a tray.

("Has Blanka gone the way of the others? Must I

return to my master Death and the easy girls of Budapest without having seen her?")

Even as a little girl, Blanka had held out the promise of glorious womanhood. She had to survive and make Life rejoice in her. Death's Coachman felt – indeed he knew – that it must be so.

And he hastened to the town from whence news of Blanka, had reached him. It was winter there, too, though spring was now chuckling in delighted mischief at snow-clad winter. Death's Coachman, whose master had given him neither horse nor carriage yet, walked along the streets on foot.

The whiteness glistened in the noonday sun when on a corner Blanka appeared, Blanka the magnificent, Blanka the all bountiful, driving a team before her, a tiny team of infants, a four-in-hand. By her side walked a lean and homely French bonne. Up front marched the four-in-hand–two little boys holding hands, three or four years of age, and behind them, two blonde girls of six or seven, with their promise of approaching womanhood, wintry all, furclad and high of spirit, with not a thought to Death's Coachman.

And Death's Coachman cracked his whip and laughed. This is his coach-and-four, these four little people, whom his former Blanka had given to another. And satisfied and all knowing now, Death's Coachman headed back to Budapest and to his master, Death.

1906

105

Bond and the Spider of Old Age

One October day old age came and with an invisible yet fine-meshed net wove a web around Bond the writer, wove it all about him. He felt nothing of this; his noble, bright, and moody eyes were as restless and searching as ever. He would have liked to heave his wide shoulders against the earth and shift it back from October to May. His legs continued strong of sinew as they tread, and his moods were in no way morbid. He felt as usual, victorious and faint hearted in turn. He could still sit down to his desk. He enjoyed great, triumphant hours. And he cursed the first written piece of paper and thought cheerfully of the mighty attenuating circumstance called Death. He could still eat rare roast beef and even had eyes for the cashier girls at the local café.

Yet on this day it was decided that Bond should never be able to wrest anything new from life, ever again. Henceforth, there would be nothing new for him. His stomach would go on digesting properly, perhaps, and women would not forsake him yet. He would even continue to write short stories. He would continue to struggle, too, between the sacred claws of eternal discontent. But on paper, there would be no more victory for him. The road to glory was now blocked; the spider's web saw to that, the old age that women had sent his way far too soon to wage war, if not against his manhood, then at least against the artistic sensitivity of his soul. The spider of old age had come, and Bond did not even suspect.

The man who had always fallen for the kisses of gentlewomen and flighty little actresses on this day, for the first time in his life, wanted a woman for his mate who could write. He was even surprised that he had not thought of this before. He fell to thinking, and in his thoughts called himself a fool. How could he have been such a dullard as to be satisfied with kisses that any ordinary man could taste? Only a fabulous, mature creature was worthy of him, a woman refined of body, artistic of soul, unfathomable as a lake, passionate and proud, the kind who on such a bright October day, whose secrets only a man of art could fathom, won't ask why you embrace him so sadly, as if you were handing out dispensation, as if you were holding a thousand different women in your arms, or as if you were attempting to give warning to the fading gardens that to approve or disapprove of life is equally unwise. Life must be studied and experienced, and its mysterious, profound reality conveyed.

So Bond set out in search of his new female companion. And the woman to whom his October journey led was happy, for she happened to be a writer. With the sweat of her brow, she spent her nights dreaming herself into an artist. And she hated Bond who, like a knight in shining armour, appeared on paper, the bloodiest of battlefields, always victorious, always in a new light. She hated Bond, the writer, with her writer's soul, but yearned for Bond, the man, with her entire vast, enamoured womanhood.

From this October day, these two travelled side by side. They travelled far and wide. They left behind a winter, spring, summer, and yet another autumn. They acted out the mighty instances of mighty artist loves. They attempted to torture each other, too, but dismayed, though mute, admitted to themselves that they had no pain to spare for each other's benefit. Always, they fished in each other's souls for subjects. They would have liked to borrow each other's eyes in order to see new things.

But from this October day, they saw nothing. The woman could not even sweat a mood or seeing half hour out of herself any more, while Bond caught nothing but mirages that flitted past him before he had a chance to sit down to his desk.

They continued to write. From time to time, they exchanged selves. And they put the final dot on their writings wearied and terrified. The woman churned out wooden, soulless imitations of one or another of Bond's old pieces, while Bond wrestled with the woman's subjects in vain. What the woman had once seen he could not tame into a semblance, even, of one of his former stories.

Meanwhile, the spider of old age continued to spin its web. And the pain came. And what pain! The woman felt that all her soul's vegetation had been trampled underfoot by the man, while whenever the woman spoke, the man thought he could hear the thud of falling graveside soil.

They lived together now just like any ordinary man and wife. Sometimes they chased life's cares away with their kisses, but only to rail at each other like hustlers when either felt that the other was standing in way of life's enjoyment.

This was a prodigious burial, a double burial, in the course of which the writer began to decline. The sleepless nights came, the hallucinations, the awful, overwhelming hours of helplessness, when he felt that he was confined to a wooden crate and he thought he could hear up on top, rapping in ridicule, those who could still see new things in life and could relish fresh, virginal moods. And was life worth living in any other way?

The hours of aging had come, the hours from which the most awesome tunes of human destitution could have been plucked, if only he knew how. But these two, once buffeted together by fate, were now incapable of leaving each other, the woman with half a soul, and the man with the mighty but dwindling heart.

They wandered around the world, they struggled, they groped. When he kissed her, the man could still recall the former women who did not smell of ink, while the woman thought of the times when she hated Bond, the writer, but yearned for Bond, the man.

What was to become of them? They had stopped asking. But as a new October day dawned, just like the one that had brought them together, they felt the strength for a confrontation of sorts, after all.

The man took the initiative.

"I shall not send you away," he said, "though I should. It is too late now, in any case. I am not good for you, I know that. So why don't you do something?"

And for a second, his soul stirred with the hope that he could be his former strong, triumphant self once again if only he could drive this woman from his side. He still did not realize that the woman had come only to finish the burial, that he was bound to her by the spider of old age, and that the passion that in his search for a woman to love had urged him to follow the scent of ink had been an unhealthy passion.

The woman's thoughts were more savage still. She felt that this man, so mighty of physique, was an impostor, not the real thing at all. He was unseeing and weak. She had been his better all along, she felt, and would have even made a better man, perhaps. Then he appeared, the faint-hearted one, to transplant his weakness into her soul. And henceforth, no real strength could issue from her either.

But Bond's eyes were bright, lovely, melancholy and restless, and she enjoyed kissing them. She could not leave him. But what was to become of them? They would be forgotten. Bond had stopped writing. When he took pen in hand, the air grew heavy with despair. Yet she, the woman, was more tormented still, and she answered Bond with their double despair.

"You should have known. Why did you have to come look for me? I hate you! I hate you! I demand my life back from you. I want my faith back, and my talent. Do something. Make a change! It is your responsibility!"

The following day, they set out on a journey. They did so in great haste, and it never occurred to either that they could have gone their separate ways. They set forth, crouching in each other's souls like two preordained sentences of death.

Soon, the sleepless nights began to dim the sparkle in the man's eyes. His strong muscles began to give, his mighty shoulders to sag. And the great dread of death came, too, bidding him to think of mortality at every turn, of the fact that he would have to go once, possibly by way of madness, or suddenly, he, a mature, mighty, dreaming piece of humanity, while this nothing of a woman with half a soul would stay behind. She would go on living. And why not? The impasse of her soul would bring her nothing but relief. She had been half a creature all along, and not much of a woman, either. But this way, she could regain her womanhood. She might get married, or she might not. But blissful and amorous, she would certainly be kissing the kind of men for whom life did not come to an end with the faltering of their pens on paper.

And so they continued on their journey with mounting hatred and mounting silence. They took a boat over sun filled days and haunting nights.

It was on such a night that a shrill cry brought the woman from her cabin and her most painful, most hate-laden thoughts. The people of the small boat were in an uproar, for someone had jumped overboard, and they could not find him in the dark.

"Him!" The suspicion struck the woman's temples like a welcome blow. "Bond! My husband!"

She did not faint, though, hard as she tried. The people around her expected her to swoon, and she would have gladly obliged them, but she could not, she simply could not.

Life flooded her puny little feline soul with unlooked for joy. A hundred times more feeling swelled up in her breast than the chambers of her heart could hold. She felt Bond by her side, the Bond of old, whom she had first known only through his always new and triumphant writings. And she could almost see Bond smiling his encouragement.

She stood alone in the early dawn, looking with tearful smiles, infinite gratitude and elation, out to sea. The elation forced her down into a rocking chair. She stroked its arm the way, not long before, she had stroked Bond's abundant stresses. And amorously, she whispered, "You dear, dear man! How I love you! How very grateful I am to you!" And she knew that her first piece of writing would be about this Bond, the Bond who had been a weak, nothing artist, really, but who loved her, the great woman writer, with all his heart. Such were her thoughts, and her soul trembled with anticipation.

1905

The Man of the Charitable Lips

The capricious yet wise gentleman was heading home. Only the drifting devil could have said where he'd been. He was never quite right in the head, and so, he spent his time wandering off the beaten path. He had money to burn. He could afford to be every bit as eccentric as he was wise. He went in search of exotic places. He liked unusual people. And he was exceedingly curious, besides, about how he would end his days.

He was travelling on a boat, having a grand time of it. He had been given a poisonous, deadly kiss on some ocean isle, and now, it was with a sense of gratification that on balmy evenings he mingled with the elegant passangers up on deck. He would have liked to squeal with laughter. If only they knew! If only they knew that a leper more leprous than any was rubbing elbows with them. How they'd toss him to the sharks! How they'd burn the last of his rags! How the faint-hearted would tremble with frenzy from the shock! How all the journalists in the world would write about the new pestilence!

Such were his thoughts. But he was not troubled. He was a man painfully considerate of his fellows, and conversant, besides, with the nature of the hell's fire he'd absorbed into his blood on the exotic ocean isle.

This had been about a hundred days before, so he'd have another forty or so days to go. Then would come the terrible, relentless hours when he'd turn into a living malignancy. But he would take the initiative. He owned magnificent pistols, and his story would be very beautiful, he knew. He had not planned it this way; not even his detractors could claim that he had come to this pass just to appear fascinating in the eyes of his fellows. He did not pretend that he was unhappy with the uncommon way he'd end his days. After all, he was already thirty, and infinitely curious to see how he would leave this vale of tears. What he'd received he'd received at the hands of fate, and by way of a kiss. It was time to head for home and visit those with whom he'd played at horses, and later, at love, where he had been a child, and a youth...

He still had forty days to come and go as he pleased. He could never kiss anyone again, of course. But what of it? The world would be a lot better off, he felt, if people didn't kiss each other, ever. If only the civilised world knew of his terrible disease, it would forget kissing altogether. For the hideous bane, worse than any biblical leprosy which was mustering itself for the awful devastation in his blood, fancied but one thing: the lips. Woe to the lips that his lips should touch; woe to anyone he might kiss!

The capricious yet wise gentleman felt proud and jubilant. He felt that he was the first of sovereigns among men. He was Death's regent on earth. All he had to do was wish it. He could get as close to anyone as he liked, and with a quick embrace, he could grab anyone's head. For just a moment he could force anyone's lips to his own. He could be the death of anyone at all. But since he knew this, he was more saintly than a saint. He saw himself enthroned at an august height above the pitiful human beetles of the world who scampered about to no avail, ignorant of what was good and worthy to take from life, and just as ignorant of what it meant to carry on one's lips the breath that extinguished it. They did not even suspect what it means when wanting to live past forty cheerful days is utterly in vain.

When he thought of them, of life's minuscule, weak and ignorant foundlings, his heart overflowed with a feeling of devout charity. "Go on, live, you feeble ones," he reflected. "You are not deserving of a privileged death. Besides, I want to go alone, in my own way. A death as august as mine has to be earned."

In the meantime, the man of the charitable lips was much admired on board ship, just as he had always been admired everywhere he went. He was as handsome as Apollo, of noble countenance, ardent yet melancholy of gaze, courageous and gallant. Many had kissed the lips on which perdition now dwelled. The eyes of the ladies aboard ship, too, sought his melancholy yet ardent eyes. One moonlit night, he even had to grab by the shoulder and toss from him a meridian-tempered, matronly beauty who, during a spontaneous scene of abandon, had nearly kissed him. At this, the capricious yet wise gentleman, Death's regent on earth, staggered a little. But his ship reached its harbour, and a speedy train conveyed him home.

Former acquaintances who saw him again now concluded that he was still not quite right in the head, while the few who had once basked in the warm proximity of his soul now nearly froze from the chill. He talked and joked with them, but the glitter of his spirit was the glitter of snowcapped mountain peaks. He spoke wittily of his adventures – he said that there were no more uncivilised lands and people to be found, and that to die is not easy anywhere, that everywhere, a kiss tastes exactly the same.

"So you're well, you're happy, you're content," he said over and over again to all who had once cuddled up to his soul and whom he wished to see one last time. He had just a few days left till he'd have to face the hell's fire about to erupt in his blood.

He visited his friends true to his intentions, and he saddened them all with his chill. But when he pressed the old, familiar hands of his male and female acquaintances, he was shaken to the core by the secret and shameful stirrings of his soul.

One man, though, he could not find, the poet whom he loved with the fullness of his heart second, perhaps, only to his wildflower. What's worse, he could not find his wildflower either, a distant female relative, untamed of blood, lovely, feminine, a girl who was yet a girl at twenty, and who was waiting expectantly for a man with unbounded love in his heart to love her as no woman had ever been loved before.

Then one day he was told, "The poet and the wildflower have found each other, and are now betrothed."

He had just one more day before he'd have to shut himself away from the society of men to go on his lonely journey, and so he hastened to them.

The young couple were sitting side by side in a love-filled salon, and when they saw the long-seen friend so dear to their hearts, their amorous folly knew no bounds. But Death's regent had fortified his soul and simply repeated, "So you're well, you're happy, you're content."

The young couple barely noticed the chill. The girl's cheeks burned with the fever of obsession. "I yearn for my darling to take me away," she panted, "I do not need to be united in the lawful, foolish way. I just want him to love me, love me, love me! I am impatient for his love."

The poet's voice was as melodious as the fizzle of burning amber dropped into cool water. "Oh, my life is just beginning. I am just about to draw my first breath. My dreams, my real dreams, are yet to be dreamt." And as he said this, his dream-beset, pallid poet's face glistened with sweat under the burden of lofty aspirations.

At this, the melancholy, ardent eyes of the capricious yet wise gentleman turned more ardent still. He felt an urge to drop to his knees. He felt that this moment was the most sublime in his life. And how perfect in timing! How happy those whom he loved! How happy!

He grabbed both their hands. He drew them to him, first the man, then the woman, and with two deliberate, long and heartfelt kisses, searing as molten lead, pressed his lips to theirs.

1905

Ten Forints' Bridegroom

One morning when St Stephen's was already bathed in the soft break of day, and on clean swept streets gay women of the night made their way home with their occasional beaus, Ten Forints' Bridegroom went in search of a quiet table. At six in the morning, it feels so good to discard one's clothes, soaked in the heady odour of the night, it feels so good to fall into bed with a sigh, and to dream heady, sweaty dreams. But Ten Forints' Bridegroom had to find his Ten Forints first, his bride, his life-sustaining Ten Forints. By noon he'd have to throw another one of his stories down the insatiable gullet of the *Journal*.* Yes, another story…

Ten Forints' Bridegroom felt a trifle sad. The café, too, where he found his table was uncomfortably musty. And since he liked to talk to himself out loud,

---

*A reference to Budapesti Napló, the newspaper where Ady was intermittently employed between 1904 and 1908. "Ten Forints' Bridegroom," published on March 30, 1905, was among his many contributions.

he addressed the slip of paper lying on the table in front of him thus: "If I don't come up with a story by noon, they will give me the boot again, and it's no good making light of such things now, is it? Still, I have nothing for you, paper, nothing. Where am I supposed to get a story all of a sudden? I have no story to suit you today!"

At this point, though, he thought of his bride, the ten forints he had to woo day in and day out in the hopes of the nuptials he knew would never come. So he asked an idle, podgy waiter with damp hair and blood-shot eyes for a new pen, and began to plow across the page. "Must I give you Zenobia, then?" he groaned, "Is there no helping it?"

His pocket watch, which he'd laid on the table, was ticking away the time. "Oh! It's nearly eight! How time flies. The piece could be ready by nine, though, and sent on its merry way, and by ten I could be lying between the sheets. But is it right to treat Zenobia thus?"

Now, then, this Zenobia was born a long time ago, a mere nothing, just the heroine of a future tale. At a time when there was no need yet to woo Fen Forints every day, her mother had been a real-life woman, and Ten Forints' Bridgroom had planned to write a novel about her. Such were his plans. In the sad world where men write, a Zenobia like this is more, sometimes, than a real-life woman, more, even, than life itself. And no Zenobia was ever more life-like than this particular Zenobia.

Zenobia was life-like because her mother had been a woman of flesh and blood; besides, she had been sustained for years, growing more and more splendid and sublime. Oh, what a novel she would make some day, Ten Forints' Bridegroom had thought at one time, a novel that would be the first piece of honesty in the world, the new gospel of the new joys and sorrows, the tender love ballad of the modern man and woman, from which the closely guarded secrets of sickly nuptial chambers would emerge, for there is nothing to hide in what a man has ever made a woman feel, even if just once, or what a woman has given a man, provided that it be an authentic letter of the alphabet of life. And Ten Forints' Bridegroom knew perfectly well that Zenobia filled the bill. In the sad world where men write, they call this a *subject trouvé*.

"When Zenobia is down on paper," Ten Forints' Bridegroom thought, "what a great day that shall be! A story larger than life. And even though one is Hungarian, she might still bring a modest fortune, not to mention a literary renaissance!"

Yes, Zenobia was going to make for an entirely new kind of story. Even in the corner of the world where he lived, Ten Forints' Bridegroom mused, people surely couldn't insist for ever on reading the bedtime stories of their tedious and dull literary tutors. Besides, his novel was ready, all it needed was pen and ink. No doubt about it, his true bride was Zenobia, Ten Forints' Bridegroom reflected, and not Ten Forints.

Just then, a handful of lively fellows sauntered into the café. Ten Forints' Bridegroom detested them heart and soul, and he did so without rhyme or reason. They came to eat breakfast. The *Journal* was their plaything. It was for their edification that tales had to be told for ten forints so that when they came again the next day, they could discover another tale in the *Journal*, and conclude how devilishly clever these strange story-telling chaps were: they had a new story for them every day.

The pen of Ten Forints' Bridegroom would not plow. If only he did not have to give them Zenobia after all! It would be unspeakable, it would be an outrage. But there was no helping it. He would have to take the story now and alter it, shrink it beyond recognition. Yet he knew that for the ten forints coming to him, he couldn't reveal so much as an honest piece of raw skin from the forehead of his real Zenobia. And to make matters worse, Ten Forints' Bridegroom reflected, he would have to mold his story to please Ten Commandment chastity.

Meanwhile, on the table the pocket watch continued to tick away the time. The waiter, too, whose damp mop of hair had dried by then, was eyeing the table where Ten Forints' Bridegroom sat with mounting impatience. Poor Ten Forints' Bridegroom! He had no other path open to a story now except the path offered by his Zenobia. It was the path on which he would have to embark.

"What is to become of Zenobia if she is to suffer such indignity?" he thought. It would mean parting with her for good. She would never become truth in print, a finished novel, for he would never be able to look his lady of fiction in the eye again for shame.

But the pocket watch continued relentless, while barely five or so black lines stood grinning up at Ten Forints' Bridegroom from his sheet of paper.

"Never mind," he told himself, "just think. You'll be sleeping in a freshly made bed soon, with your limbs freed of clothing, though by the time you rise again, your ten forints will be gone."

The morning sunlight streamed into the café. "Come, come, Zenobia, let's get on with it, and a good riddance to you," Ten Forints' Bridegroom urged. "What were you? The new woman turned masculine in her sexuality? Well, now you shall be a woman heading haughtily to a lover's trist. But your lover will not be your true lover, Zenobia, and the story will end with you going back to your lawfully wedded husband amid tears. This is what will become of you, Zenobia. But at least your story shall be read tomorrow over breakfast."

There was no time to lose. Driven by the need to get into bed and sleep secure of his ten forints, Ten Forints' Bridegroom skipped over his sheets of paper. He knew he would never conjure up Zenobia, the real Zenobia, in his innermost soul, ever again. He would be too disgusted with himself. Mocked, rejected and ignobly steeped in lies, he was now sending Zenobia the way of the others.

Ten Forints' Bridegroom was the only one left in the café. He had finished. He summoned the waiter. He stood and rushed away from the wicked corner where his table stood. His head whirled as if with the knell of funeral bells. On this day he had betrayed his own soul, betrayed it thoroughly. He was overwhelmed with blind fury. The batch of paper that had devoured Zenobia scorched his palm. He felt miserable. There was no other human being in the place except for the waiter, the newspaper dispenser, the provider of breakfast. And so, in a hoarse, maddened whisper, Ten Forints' Bridegroom dumped all his bitterness on him.

"Scoundrel! I loathe you! I loathe you!"

By the time the red-eyed waiter recovered from the shock, Ten Forints' Bridegroom was gone in search of his bride, his ten forints. He ran on and on so he could fall into bed, and so he could run away from himself, and into the arms of a heady, sweaty, daytime dream.

1905

Schoolmaster Barrel Gun

When the schoolmaster came back from the shore of Lake Balaton in late August, all who saw him were amazed. He was a new man, a changed man, he could even smile. He smiled and addressed his sad, frail and ageing wife as Mamma, and once in a while, after the midday meal or dinner, he'd stroke the heads of his three grown daughters.

These were unlooked-for events at home. At the age of fifty, the schoolmaster, the formidable, disagreeable schoolmaster, had mellowed at last. He was himself aware that he had mellowed, and was not ashamed to own up to it; he even made up his mind to chase his old memories away. Though life was mean and contemptible, men were ignoble and society worm-infested, like an unripe bunch of figs, a gathering of little worth, the Balaton was lovely and majestic, startling and hypnotic, a holy, tranquil sea even in its fury. And how many teachers and other types of men there were, the schoolmaster thought, who had never so much as set their eyes on the Balaton and their own more felicitous souls, even at the age of fifty!

For six straight weeks, the schoolmaster wandered around the lake alone and unfettered – unfettered for the first time in his life, freed of a disagreeable, pitiful gentleman whom the younger generation, the teachers' room and the town all referred to as Schoolmaster Barrel Gun. This schoolmaster was a frightful, detestable fellow, of which, sadly enough, he was himself aware – aware that he was like this, this frightful and detestable. But he had his excuses. He knew his past and he knew his present, and he had his explanations.

To begin with, he was born into a family of carpenters where, when his father was doing well, he kept an assistant, an entire assistant. Then, during his unavoidable and wretched school days, he sobered up, because everyone said that it was the thing to do. They made him believe that he must make his mark in the world, must make a gentleman of himself, must even live like one. And with violent, near mythical fury, the schoolmaster considered that he had not reached manhood as other, happier youths had done. He could not take carefree holidays, he could not play along the roadside; he had curbed all of his youthful passions.

He starved and studied the requisite number of years, passed exam after exam, and ran up a considerable debt into the bargain. But more than any debt, he was tortured by a temptation comprised in part of the frustration of what he felt to be his middle-class obligation on the one hand, and by his physical and psychological need on the other.

"You must get yourself married," his family and the memories of his race urged, and so did the cheerlessness of his young life.

Needless to say, no decision could redeem or make amends for the momentous mistakes of the past. And so, when just an assistant teacher and in debt up to the tips of his thinning hair, the schoolmaster entered into matrimony. He ran off with the girl, though he needn't have bothered, for she was the daughter of an impoverished clerk, diminutive, gentle and frail, a little nobody who had everything to gain if she went off with the schoolmaster, and precious little to hope for if she did not. And so she went, and they made each other miserable. Bidding their time, they struggled against a tide of mounting debts. They had just about come to loathe each other, too, when the little ones began to come in quick succession, three of whom died, thank God, and only three survived.

Only three survived, just three little girls, and the mother of the girls, and the debts. The mounting hatred of the schoolmaster against all those who did not have to know the bitter suffering that was his lot prevailed as well. His loathing prevailed, too, against all and sundry, but especially against life's innocents, the children. The schoolmaster hated no one as much as his own pupils, for their eyes were bright, and they invariably had to carry a lighter burden than he had to carry at one time.

*

All his friends wanted the schoolmaster to go on a real holiday at last, a real getaway. That he was not a bad sort, really, but that the unrelenting hand of fate would make him bad, every clear-sighted man could see. So they tried to save him before it was too late. They procured a small and not too painful loan for him, and instructed him to be idle and carefree without a moment's delay, as if he were just starting out in life. He'd have plenty to face later anyway, he'd need all this strength: his eldest daughter was twenty-five, and his youngest eighteen. He would have to get them married; they expected it, and it was questionable whether they would find anyone half as crazy about them as the schoolmaster had been about their mother.

But through its magical nature the Balaton worked an astonishing change in the schoolmaster, and after a long fast, his schoolboy feelings surged up in his heart. At Balatonfüred he even followed in the wake of a sixteen-year-old girl, a total stranger, from a hundred paces, until he came to his senses and was overcome with shame. At Földvár, where he had gone on an excursion, he joined the company of vacationing schoolboys from good families, and gave vent to the high spirits that by all rights he should have given vent to some thirty-odd years before. Life is beautiful, he told himself one night in a fever of excitement, but you mustn't be born the son of a poor carpenter. And then you mustn't let life with its profuse gifts pass you by, and you mustn't be petty minded either. And if your debts mount up, you should at least have the good sense not to marry a pretty face. And if all this should go wrong just the same, you should be able to keep your memories alive as a last resort, and learn to make the best of a bad deal.

It was thanks to such episodes and finely tuned reflections that the schoolmaster resumed his former life in the small town where he lived. It was pursuant upon such a felicitous emotional crisis that he took account of his past and present, of himself, and those who belonged to him. "If there is hope of a year of semi-unhappiness," he declared, like a new creed, "one must ignore the fact that for fifty years one has been totally miserable."

*

In obedience to his habitual sense of duty, by late August Schoolmaster Barrel Gun dropped in at school every day, sometimes even twice a day. Then one fine, sunny and magnificent morning, a dashing youth entered the teachers' room and asked to see the schoolmaster. He had a letter addressed to him, and as he handed it over, his eyes looked big, bold, and very bright.

"Father would also like," he added when the school-master stopped perusing the letter, "for me to find lodgings with the family of his dear old friend for the year."

"But why have you switched schools before your final exams, Son?" the schoolmaster asked with the kind of ill humour that was so much a part of his nature before he'd seen the Balaton.

"Because when I was in the seventh form, I had a nasty run of bad luck, and inside of a year, I had to transfer schools twice. At Székely-Szent-Mihály I fell in love with the headmaster's daughter, and at Nagy-Nádas, I enjoyed myself rather more than I should have."

The tall, handsome boy said this with such an innocent expression on his face that the schoolmaster was won over. The boy's father, a big landowner, high spirited, idle and clever, had been his school fellow. He liked and respected his schoolmate, the present schoolmaster, very much, for he had been the best of the lot. And now, the one-time star student thought affectionately of his old schoolmate, the idle but kind-hearted Aváry.

"Your father lives in Budapest, I believe?" he asked the boy with a new youthfulness. "He's a ministerial counsellor, is he not? And isn't your mother an Iharossy girl?" And the schoolmaster thought with awe of the schoolboy ideal to whom he dared make no overtures, not even in thought.

"Father is a titular under-secretary of state now, and always speaks of you with affection. But Mother died three years ago. Father's only wish now is to have me start out in life from under your wings."

The boy's eyes sparkled as he said the word 'life', while the schoolmaster felt emotions entirely new to him.

"Does your father know that I have children? Does he know that I have three grown daughters?"

"Yes, Sir. And he says that for a wild boy like me, the best reform school is the society of young ladies."

The schoolmaster fell silent, resorted to some quick mental calculations, then addressed the youth again.

"Your father was a very good friend. So, for one year, I shall regard his son as my own. But you need take no notice of my daughters for five or six years at least, do you understand?

"No, of course not," said the stylishly dressed youth, looking defiantly at the schoolmaster with his huge, earnest eyes. "But if I should, no final examination, father, schoolmaster or former sweetheart would make the least difference. Besides, I am here for you to put my life on the right track."

From the boy's lips the schoolmaster seemed to hear the unaccustomed melody of his own lost youth. And the once formidable and cruel schoolmaster, now newly gentle, meekly took the boy home with him. He now felt that there was a lake gentler still and more sacred than the Balaton — the lake of life. After all, life had delivered the son of the union of his unattainable female ideal and wealthy school fellow right into his hands. He could even make the boy fall in love with one of his daughters if he liked. But he won't do it, he concluded. He will watch over this boy. He will set no hardship in the way of his enjoyment of life, his road to happiness. "How happy this boy is," murmured Schoolmaster Barrel Gun, who could now see as clear as day that in this life, unhappiness and happiness are equally disinterested.

1909

Zenobia's Village

Since Zenobia's time, in a small village by the River Maros, the peasant children go around in boots, Hungarians and Romanians alike, even on St George's Day. In this same village, a girl child brings cause for rejoicing, and in school, the boys brag about their older sisters. These sisters live in Budapest, Arad and Nagyvárad, and even at far greater distances.

This, then, is the way of the village since Zenobia's time. During a damp, deadly spring of yore, children dropped like flies in the village. Only Zenobia's little brother was spared by the pestilent fever, for Zenobia had sent the boy a pair of leather boots from Kolozsvár. That particular spring and Zenobia's boots opened the eyes of men. They learned that a girl child is a great blessing. Ever since, whoever can do so sends his daughter away. Destitute, miserable cotters dwell hereabouts; why shouldn't the girls bring back a little blessing from the world so full of riches?

Zenobia is still living, the first among women in

her village. Back then, she came home and was married as is right and proper. She has numerous grandchildren now, and her family regards the village from the vantage point of a certain modest degree of prosperity. And Zenobia hands out her advice with love; likewise, the people listen to her with love.

But let no man malign this village and sit in judgment upon it. Ever since her return, Zenobia has been the model of the good and faithful wife. Only in scattered hamlets of the grim Scottish hills and in obscure corners of Holland is virtue held in such high esteem. If they are fair, girls soon dream about their duty to go out into the world. And woe to the maid who comes to grief in Zenobia's village! For there are many fair girls in Zenobia's village, where a touching solemnity sits upon the maidens' cheeks. Once, such alabaster girls would have been destined for the convent.

The young men of the village have grown resigned to their fate long ago. For them, the girls are touch-me-nots. Only the homely are avaible to them, but they wait patiently for the pretty ones to return.

With time, these girls managed to spread the veneer of a comic, cockeyed sort of gentility over their village. The people learned about new things. They saw life from new perspectives. New, almost courtly virtues were thus transplanted here, by the region of the River Maros, since Zenobia and that certain pair of little boots. Fancy, stylish and adorned in silks, one or another of the girls would sometimes come home for a visit. These girls were as untouchable as the vestal virgins of old; to propose marriage to them before it was time was an unpardonable sin.

And so, the girls came and went. Those who lived at far off places sent presents to their families. They sent money, clothing, and many other things besides. The post office had its hands full with the village, which now lived in the turbulent stream of modern life, all because of its daughters, its good daughters.

For the girls were good in Zenobia's village. They honoured their fathers, their mothers, sisters, and brothers. They wept quickly, with an easy emotionality. They never turned against the order of things. Those girls whom their parents sent away to support them went without a word. Above their heads, one could almost see the divine halo of weighty obligations and great sacrifices. And when they returned to their village, they found their mates, and loved them as was proper, and they presented them with children.

Meanwhile, Zenobia had grown much advanced in years. But she was not afraid of death, for in her heart nestled that proud quiescence which makes death welcome to the true reformer. Perhaps she even felt the approach of death, for it pained her that she would not get to see Maria again. Maria was the loveliest of all her granddaughters, a winsome, alabaster adolescent destined to follow one of her older sisters out into the world.

Then one spring, as Zenobia was sunning herself on the lawn of her garden, Maria appeared before her.

"Grandmother, I wish to be married!"

The ground trembled. Pollution descended upon the face of the earth. Griefstricken and mute, Zenobia began to weep.

"Whom would you marry, you depraved child?

"The man I love."

Maria was given no supper that night. Maria's grandmother, mother, and all her female relations cried. The men cursed and looked at her with contempt.

The news spread through the village like wildfire. The women folk came and admonished Maria, but to no avail. Stubborn and mute, she stood up to their entreaties.

"I will get married all the same. I will belong to the man I love!"

Zenobia's village was up in arms. Letters came from girls living at great distances, threatening, pleading letters. But in the end, Maria prevailed. She moved to her lover's shack. Hardly anyone attended their wedding. Shrouded in silence, the village mourned.

Then, on the night of the wedding, the village sat in judgment. The tongues of flame reached them, and scorched, Maria and her husband fled.

For Zenobia's village, which would not forgive disloyalty and depravity, invoked a curse upon them. The curse bore fruit. A son was born to Maria who, with her husband, was very poor. Another damp, pestilent spring came, and Maria's little boy died, for the poor child had no boots.

1906

The Kiss

from the tales of an aging journalist

Inscribed on a tombstone you can read, *"Here dwells Rozália Mihályi. She lived twenty-six years. Peace be to her ashes. I will go and be with Christ, for that is best beyond all things."*

Rozália Mihályi – may the good earth be kind to her – she was an insignificant lass of the theatre while she lived. She dyed her red hair, as I have since learned, but her lips were naturally ruddy. She laughed loudly and merrily, though not with a light heart; but because the gentlemen of the theatrical board liked their chorus girls that way. She was the disinherited daughter of a Lutheran minister, and death terrified her only because she would not get to play in the operetta *Touch Me Not*. For five years running she had been promised the part by managers, directors, even critics. *Touch Me Not* cost her more kisses than love, money, and her toilette combined. Yet she died, poor thing, with her great ambition unfulfilled, and she flooded her death bed at the hospital with tears.

The other paraphernalia of death did not concern

Rozália Mihályi, for she was a reckless woman. Now she lies at Arad or Kassa, I will not say where, or for how long. I never met Rozália Mihályi, yet no woman looms larger in my life; the story, too, that I am about to relate is a story about her, small yet deep and profound as any mountain lake. The real heroine of this story, then, is Rozália Mihályi, who is now with Christ, for that is best beyond all things.

*

I had already asked Marcella Kun eight times to kiss me and say that she held me dear. Being an aspiring second primadonna, she could turn it to her advantage. After all, I wrote the reviews.

She was a dark-haired girl, clever and open-minded; moreover, she probably did not find me repulsive. At most, my embraces would not overjoy her; and then, too, she saw the trouble ahead. I was a most virile lad at the time and made no bones about the fact that I was a veritable madman in my love-making. Let her whom I chose for myself also go mad and scream with joy, and let her boast of it afterwards.

Marcella Kun was right to fear this, she who had contrived to keep her porcelain complexion white till then, during and in spite of all embraces. There were times when I told her what I had dreamt about her, and that I considered her the most desirable cushion in Creation, the resting place, the haven, the harbour where a man should rest, and where he would willingly rest for ever.

In short, Marcella Kun was afraid of me, and because she was afraid of me, I had free access to the hotel room where she lived. She admitted me into her presence even when she was taming her wild, coarse black hair with a variety of combs. By degrees I won the right to hold this strong, black hair, which mocked her delicate frame, up to my cheek. If, however, the proximity of Marcella Kun's neck, shoulders, and indeed her entire little body intoxicated me unduly, I was given a chiding.

"Would it satisfy you, Sir, to ravish me, body and soul, and hear me call you a rogue? Would you have such plundered success, such loveless love? Well, would you?"

At such times I trembled and wept; and above all, I wept because I was such a foolish, weak man. A woman like her occasions different treatment. But I craved another kind of woman in her, better, generous, and infatuated, whereas her eyes, dark Marcella Kun's eyes, were blue, cold, unfeeling, bad blue eyes. They had never turned up in their sockets, I felt, they had never been stunned with love. "Just you wait, you bad, blue eyes, just you wait! I am after your fire."

I promised myself I'd end this farce. After all, I am no male Marcella Kun. I did not learn the ways of love so I would know what love was, but so I could consume it and burn myself with it, as is only right. And so, one fine day I said to Marcella Kun, "Marcie" – that was my petname for her – "tomorrow afternoon you will admit no one but me. I will have exclusive entry. You will receive no one else tomorrow afternoon."

Such mighty preparations and preprogrammed bravery, though, I recommend only to men with fine, barbaric constitutions. My own mighty pre-arrangements and pretended courage resulted in a cursed, demented night. I was a most weary fellow the next day, and in the afternoon, knocked on Marcella Kun's door only to save face.

She wept. No matter. Her bad blue eyes grew soft and moist, and so blue, they were almost brown. When I entered she grew faint and was unable to stand, and – there could be no doubt about it – at that moment she even hated me. I would have liked to cradle the diminutive, pale-black, foolish little thing in my lap and rock her gently like a baby, to sing to her in a melancholy voice so she could sleep, so I could sleep, for the night had been a bad one. I would have liked to sing a lullaby something like this, "Marcie, little Marcie, let us not kiss. What's the use of kissing? Marcie, little Marcie, I will tuck you in, and we will touch cheeks and feel our tears mingle like two silly infants. Marcie, little Marcie, all I want is to cry with you today, to howl with all my might."

But man is a pitiful creature who must love even when he feels no real inclination for it. So I sat down by Marcella Kun's side and with great, pretended passion, proceeded to bite her lip. Her sole response was to insist on the advisability of pressing a per-fectly clean white linen handkerchief to where it bled.

Feeble and sad, she stood up, and when she had found the handkerchief, came back, but as if she had just received a fatal wound and were heading for Calvary.

I unpinned her hair, she suffered it, but all the while she spoke in the devout manner of old women telling their rosaries.

"I know you men. I know how futile it is to talk, cry, or plead. So be it. But I do not want this thing. It brings me no joy. It is painful. However, you are all of a feather. Dearly have I paid every time I have had anything to do with a man, especially one whom I loathed, but I had to, the one who wrecked my body, too."

I heard yet heard not what she was saying, for I was kissing her slippers by then. Man is a pitiful creature who is capable of love even if a moment before he had no appetite for it. And so I felt compelled to seek out her eyes, to gaze up at her face – and thought I had surely gone mad. For Marcella Kun's eyes were no longer blue but nearly black, her hair was red, her lips were like rubies. She was other than herself, and for a moment or two, we were both clearly bewitched.

(Of course, today I know that Rozália Mihályi had come to work this witchcraft. I recognize her perfectly from the descriptions of those whom I had encountered and interviewed since, those who knew her very well, Rozália, the grandest, the mightiest woman in my life.)

I did not have my fill of Marcella Kun that afternoon,

but I did not yet crave the memory of her kisses, fine as they were, I still say so today, I dare say so. Of course, they were mournful and sad, too, whereas men of my disposition go in pursuit of kisses expressly to be delivered of sadness. I nevertheless saw her again when in my blood our kiss had already become like a goblet that remembered too late to overflow. My blood sprouted roses, blazing, wrathful, abundant roses of love.

(Horrible! Horrible! I can see it again; again, Marcella Kun was like the descriptions of Rozália Mihályi. Again, we embraced, but now I loved a chimera, not her, a red haired, full-lipped, dark eyed Other. Marcella Kun was there, too, but Rozália Mihályi was far more substantially there. And someone else seemed to have joined us as well, someone all three of us loathed.)

Marcella Kun bowed her head, kissed me and said, "It is all the same now. You asked for it. I warned you!"

I asked her whom she had in mind the time that her talk fell on my deaf ears.

"I was in Győr at the time, and he was a journalist," she said, "and the manager's friend. He said I must, he'll have me thrown out otherwise, and there would be no place for me anywhere in the country."

Marcella Kun even told me the name of the man, and I was overjoyed, as you can imagine! A zero, a non-entity, oh! It was well worth receiving the souvenier of one of his amorous adventures into my blood!

I thought of ways not to take it too much to heart; it was all so singular, so fascinating, after all. But malignant and spiteful, my health, like Job's health by now, raged with resentment. ("Whose kiss has come between us, pernicious and noxious, between myself and Marcella Kun? There is someone here I must go in search of, there is someone I have yet to find. Great secrets lie hidden here. After much exertion I manage to obtain a kiss, and what happens? Someone who has beaten me to the mark goes and poisons my kisses.")

Marcella Kun did not lament overmuch with me. On the contrary, she seemed gratified. What is more, at this moment I wanted her so desperately, had they brought me the purest vestals of Aphrodite, I could not have cared less. In thought I craved just one thing, to be outrageously wicked.

"Well, my virginal angel, will you reveal the whereabouts of your lover, the man so worthy of you?"

She was not shocked. She was not furious. She just told me where he was to be found.

("I'm off. I'm off in pursuit of the scoundrel," I thought. "After all, what should a man keep a track of if not his own kisses? Let me learn who had sent him to Marcella Kun, so Marcella Kun should later tell me that she had exchanged a fatal kiss.")

I had heard about him. He was a journalist, a Hungarian from Pest, ignorant, mean, and Jewish. He talked big at first, but a couple of good slaps in the face, and he turned meek as a lamb.

147

"You knew Marcella Kun. But who came before her, you impudent scoundrel, you cur?"

A submissive confession followed. He beat his breast and presently divulged a name: Rose Mihályi.

"Rose Mihályi?" I said. "Red hair? Ruby lips? Dark eyes?"

"Yes, yes, in Arad, once. But you're a man, just like me. Try to understand."

"So it is the chorus girl Rozália Mihályi, is it? Good bye, and may you be damned!" ("I know this woman, I have seen her many times while I embraced that other. Just you wait, Rozália Mihályi, you will be called to account when we meet!")

And so, I set out for the town where Rose Mihályi reputedly lived. After all, a kiss is no trifling matter and if a man's kiss has proven unlucky, he should at least find out with whom and by whom he'd come into such a mighty, melancholy, yet ultimately just brotherhood.

I would be lying if I did not hasten to add that during this painful phase of my life, when I played her tormentor, I loved Marcella Kun more than ever. I should also mention, perhaps, that precisely at this juncture, Marcella Kun's bad blue eyes were beginning to turn into the loveliest of doe-like eyes for the benefit of someone else. But I was preoccupied. I had to find Rose Mihályi. I had to find Rozália. For man is a pitiful creature who does not always get from a kiss what he had bargained for. ("Perhaps this is the great inducement to the human kiss," I philosophised on the way. "Still, it is not right, not right at all." Yet, strange as it may seem, at this time I regarded women with red hair, bright red lips and dark eyes with special attention, even on the train.)

I won't reveal whether it was Arad or Kassa, but arrive I did, and mightily pleased with myself in this curious hunt for the viper of my embraces, I made inquiries after Rozália Mihályi.

"Let me see. It is March, so she must have died at the beginning of February," said the old cashier at the theatre. He winked slyly and added that there are far prettier girls than she in the chorus.

I felt like a child deprived of its party favour.

"But it is her I want, it is red hair I want. I want Rozália Mihályi."

The old man sent for the porter, who told me in which row of the graveyard Rozália lay. And to put my mind at ease, he whispered in my ear, "She was a good girl, mind you, and pretty. But poor child, she died of a nasty disease."

("It is no use continuing the search for the one who has sent me a message by way of a bad kiss," I thought. "I cannot talk with Rozália Mihályi, I cannot extort a confession from her. I can do but one thing: I can turn Rozália Mihályi into the Muse of Life, into the Muse of Love. She was unfamiliar enough to me for that, but burst into my life with sufficient force. Besides, there is no telling how long I would have to look for the person who had sent me a sad message about love through Marcella Kun as a reward for my male animality.")

149

The next morning, which proved to be bright and sunny, I took a beautiful wreath to the graveyard for Rozália Mihályi's tomb. That is where I read, *"Here dwells Rozália Mihályi. She lived twenty-six years. Peace be to her ashes. I will go and be with Christ, for that is best beyond all things."*

Oh, Lord, and so it is! But what about those who cannot go? They must proceed to live as long as they can with the thing that had killed Rozália Mihályi. Red hair, ruby lips, dark eyes. I see them now, I shall continue to see them all the days of my life. And I shall continue to kiss, too, though now I know that the human kiss is merely a way of sending a message, and that at times this message is very, very sad.

1908

Stella Morbida in Paris

1.

To this day I do not know what had come over me at the time, but I broke into a run and before I knew it found myself in Madame d'Alta's celebrated, exotic *salon*. It was May, a May pieced together from bits of blues and reds, the kind that can quicken the blood like this only along the banks of the Seine. In Paris, once you've sold your soul to the city and the Devil, you become fully conscious of every little thing that has anything whatsoever to do with your life, anything that has the least design upon it – or is about to have. Whether joy or jeopardy lurk in wait, Paris will whisper it in your ear in good time, then spur you on to meet it.

Madame d'Alta, the celebrated Pythia, the most sought after and heartless fortuneteller in Paris, kept me waiting, which was only to be expected. But this way, at least, I had ample time at my disposal to learn why I had felt compelled to purchase foolish prophecies for one gold Louis. I had spotted the portrait of the woman who had driven me there, taken in Athens, if my memory serves me right, a brash, calculated photograph, the letters on it still practically wet with ink. And that curious name, too, strung together by a highly excitable hand from highly excitable characters: Stella Morbida. It was the likeness of a woman who at first glance seemed like a child of ten, then presently a fairy tale princess saddened and wisened into womanhood before her time, a creature descended of an indeterminate, pallid, lovely old race, an exotic and remote type, a witch who had strayed from some distant land, dangerous, and best avoided.

"Madame," I said as I wrenched my hand from hers while she was telling my fortune, "it is not my palm or fortune you should be concerned with, that's not why I'm here. I'm here because I felt the call of something or someone whose portrait I have just discovered in your grand salon. It stands on a small table, in the company of a little elephant amulet. It is the dedicated portrait of a woman. Who is she? When did she come here? What does she want with Paris? And what does she want with me?"

Madame d'Alta grabbed my hand again, looked into my eyes, and answered in a very dry voice.

"Indeed I hardly know who that woman is or from where she's come to Paris, where I dropped myself like a bird exhausted in mid-flight. But I see that she wants nothing from you. You might meet. After all, Paris is so small. But that will be the end of it. We come to this town in droves, strangers to the last man, drawn by the glitter, and born to be burnt.

You're like this yourself, and so am I, perhaps, and so is Stella Morbida. All those whose photographs or calling cards you saw in my salon are assuredly like this."

2.

The following day I strolled along the grand boulevard with a young Romanian painter. I was feeling less excited by then. I can't recall the subject of our conversation, but all at once, the Romanian grabbed my arm in something like dread.

"Look! See that woman? She's coming this way, headed right for us, with Prince Bozhidar."

The Romanian painter knew Prince Bozhidar, but I – I knew the woman. She had been the one who had confounded me so the other day with the intimation of her presence. It was Stella Morbida, whose portrait I had discovered the day before in Madame d'Alta's *salon*. With her frivolous, blue, Empire-style toilette, her restless, untamed yet majestic presence, she'd have embarrassed a far greater city, even, than Paris. Wherever they went – for we set off after them right away – a traffic jam ensued, commotion abounded, mighty, lightning loves were engendered, and automobiles ran over unsuspecting pedestrians.

By the time we reached the Place de la Concorde in pursuit of Stella Morbida, the Romanian painter was weeping and sighing.

"I must meet her, or die! I shall die unless she leaves Paris this instant!"

153

As it happened, we did not have long to suffer, for in just two days, we were introduced to Stella Morbida. A German or Austrian sculptor gave a not too distinguished dinner, where Stella Morbida was among the guests. A most unlikely assemblage of people they were from the foreign colonies, a frantic, aimless lot of low artist types, but from them we learned that Stella Morbida was the daughter of a wealthy Greek gentleman from Macedonia. Her mother had been Bulgarian, her husband Romanian, and the lover from whom she'd fled to Paris, a Turk. She had had a French governess, had been to Paris before, and was interested in all things printed in French characters. She was the kind of Parisienne we foolish strangers pine for back home.

During the dinner and the night that followed, Stella Morbida almost drove me out of my mind. My only consolation was that the Romanian painter was suffering, too, though Stella Morbida took far more heed of him than of me. Instead of laughing like the others, she preferred to strike efficacious and langorous poses. Clearly, the other women attending the soirée would have liked to strangle her.

3.

For a whole month I slept, woke, and generally conducted myself like a lunatic. I avoided the company I usually kept, for I wanted no news, even, of Stella Morbida. Let her drive all of Paris to distraction just as long as she leaves me in peace, because I could not bear it!

But a month later, the Romanian painter paid me

a visit. He was pale, but so calm that to look at him was worth more than two portions of bromine to me. "Oh," I thought, "I hope I shall have the forbearance not to ask any questions!" But the Romanian volunteered to speak of his own accord, and so we went for a walk.

We walked on and on. It was a glorious June day, and as a matter of course, we found ourselves on the Boulevard. I gaped at Paris, which for a month I had not been able to look at with sober, steady eyes. How charming, how peaceful and calm it seemed! There was no danger lurking in wait anywhere.

At first, I did not pay much heed to what the painter was saying. I began to listen only bye and bye, and even then, what I heard seemed to have precious little to do with me any more. It was more like a dream, remote, incredible, alien.

"She's gone." It sounded to me like the last words of the Redeemer on the cross, and it was clearly incumbent upon me to know whom he meant.

"She's gone. Can't you tell by looking at this great city, at the world and at myself that she is gone? She was an awful woman. She struck up an acquaintance with everyone in Paris worth knowing. She came to me, too, the other day, shaken by hysterical fits of weeping. "I am here," she said, "because I have never been happy for two days in all my life. Two days. I want to be happy for just two days, understand? Give me two days of happiness, then do with me as you like, for I refuse to go back home!"

"And how long did you stay with the poor thing?" I asked, now fully allerted.

"At the end of the first day, it was because of me, she said, that she had to come to Paris; I was her ultimate happiness. The next morning we breakfasted together, at noon we parted, and in the afternoon, she left Paris."

"Are you quite certain that she is not in Paris still?" I inquired. "That she is gone for good?"

"I am certain. I received a letter from her yesterday, written in Belgrade. It was heartless, aloof – and beautiful."

"But what did this odious woman, this adventuress want?" I asked.

The Romanian made no answer, and so we continued walking in silence for another hour or two. Paris was miraculously calm, and so were our hearts, bodies, and minds. We were happy, happy that someone had left Paris, someone who brought desire to every man, but fulfillment to none.

1908

The Blinded Muse

Victor, the forty-year-old, melancholy youth, was visited by true happiness at last. It was autumn, the season for miraculous revelations. The tropical trees of the Garden of Luxembourg had not yet been removed, and hoar frost had not yet appeared. In the sunlight, the water of the Seine seemed to be ablaze. And he, the forty-year-old, melancholy youth, roamed the streets of sun-drenched Paris as if he were Summer incarnate, stirred in its affections and fulfilled, whose blessing the radiant world awaits as it gradually slips into winter.

Never before had it been granted to him to walk with such a light step. Never before had he beheld the countenance of true happiness. Since the time that his heart had first constricted in the manner of those who in this earthly existence cannot sit down to the feast of life in peace, he had been drifting and searching. He had been like one come from a very great distance, laden with memories and much wearied, and who is with us for a brief instant only before he must continue his journey into the infinite beyond.

But now, true happiness was here; Phryne* was here, she who is Woman incarnate to all foolish artists, our companion of a single, yet of a thousand shapes, Phryne, who never takes her eyes off us, Phryne the Immortal, who never wants to catch our eyes.

When Victor reached the Place Concorde, he had a sudden inspiration.

"It is not right," he reflected, "that I should go without company. After all, from now on, everything will be different. I have already told Dora I would be bringing guests. I am going to send off telegrams right away, and order fresh oysters and champage."

Fulfilling his own desires like a *grand seigneur*, Victor, whom true happiness had affianced at last, headed home. Sharp and crimson, the last rays of the autumn sun buffeted his retreating figure as he disappeared through the front gate. Then, with the approach of night, the lamps were lit in all the rooms of the fourth floor. And humming to herself, Dora set the table in Victor's atelier.

She had hardly finished when they began arriving – the knotty-haired Russian, whose only purpose in life was to refute Tolstoy in verse, the ruddy Norwegian, who carved images of despair into stone – the kind of exotic gathering that had to know better than anyone what it means when a man is visited by

---

*Phryne (4th c. B.C.) was a Greek courtesan and the lover of the great sculptor Praxiteles. She was the model for several Aphrodites, including the famous Aphrodite of Cnidus, now at the Louvre.

true happiness, the kind of assemblage that could have gathered together like this only in a Parisian hideaway. Besides, here, in the autumn night, where the barriers cutting Neuilly off from the rest of Paris were just a stone's throw away, in this tranquil street, on the uppermost storey of a shabby tenement, ecstasy was in the making.

Dora, whose milky complexion had been set afire even before the champagne, occupied the head of the table. She was loud, and periodically broke into nervous gales of laughter. She wove her speech of five different languages. But the guests were grave, and Victor, who had been visited by true happiness at last, was moved beyond words as he looked at them. The atelier was thick with incense and groaning under the weight of exotic rugs. Dark draperies hung upon the walls, and mysterious figures loomed on the walls and easels in every obscure corner – the mighty tragedies of the soul of a forty-year-old, melancholy youth made incarnate.

There were pictures and more pictures everywhere, and on them stood all the glitter and all the gloom of a prodigious struggle; pictures that had gone unfinished, intimations of the nagging secrets and the incomprehensibility of Life. Blood, sweat, and tears, they were all there; and yet, they had nothing to say, these paintings that had laughed to scorn so many fitful hours of fevered inspiration.

But across from the table, adorned with a live chrysanthemum and looking as if she were about to pass through the threshold of some hidden arbour

159

of flowers and delights stood Phryne, gazing at the company. Her hair, too, was bedecked with flowers; her very nakedness seemed flowery. She even lookedcapable of speech.

"It is not nice," she seemed to be saying, "that you poets and artists have neglected me for so long. You have been going about your business for hundreds and hundreds of years, yet you attempt to find me in frail female bodies that wither even before they bloom. Have you, then, not felt my eyes upon you? Since the beginning of time, poets and artists have been restless because I gaze upon them. Thank you, you forty-year-old melancholy youth, for finding me at last!" Victor could even hear Phryne speak. He glanced joyfully at Dora, and he glanced at his guests. And together, they all glared at Phryne.

Victor was the first to break the silence.

"Look at her eyes! It is for these eyes that I have lived. And now I am so happy, I could die. For what more could a man want? My exertions have given radiance to the first pair of true eyes, eyes that could have never throbbed in a skull of mere flesh and bone. Only these eyes are genuine, for in them dwells Life in its fullness. It is these eyes that have made us melancholy. It is these eyes that have haunted us ever since the birth of song, chisel, bow, and brush. It is these eyes that force us to exchange our Doras for new ones over and over again, losing our faith in them even before we have made them a gift of it. It is because of this pair of eyes that we fear happiness, for when happiness is about to take its

start, we already know that a funeral will be conse-
quent upon it. And so, we do not even give happiness a chance. But I have broken the curse. Oh, how
often has dawn found me standing in front of this
canvas! And now, look! I have conjured her up, I
have conjured up Phryne! Fling open the windows
and let the perfume of incense waft out into this
blessed autumn night."

The Norwegian broke into a song, like a hymn.
But Dora sat silent and defiant across from Phryne.
The men raised their glasses, and to them all it
seemed that Phryne had joined them in their
singing, her exquisite body swaying to the rhythm of
a pagan dance that was quiet and intimate, and that
her eyes had become moist with tears.

"Did you never love me, then?" Dora asked as she
leaned closer to Victor after the last strains of the
hymn-like song had died away.

Victor answered in the tremulous, liberal manner
of those in ecstasy.

"I have loved you very much, and love you still,
for it is what she wanted. I love you, and I love those
that have come before you. I have loved all my
Doras. It is not your fault, or the fault of your sisters,
that you cannot bring true happiness."

"And that painted canvas?" Dora asked.

"That?... Yes. Just look at her eyes!"

And all glances were directed at Phryne's
wonderful eyes, those two holy vessels of untold
secrets.

The hours fled by, and through the open window,

the chilly dawn came to greet them. They were drinking punch. Victor sat in a rocking chair, smoking a Havanna, and through the smoke, gulping down the September air into his parched lungs. But on his face glowed the pallour of the most sacred of fatigues, the ecstatic fatigue of fulfillment.

Without taking his eyes off Phryne, Victor called to the knotty-haired Russian, who knew how to write poetry.

"Ivan, write a pagan verse for my Phryne. I feel like a king. I shall give you whatever you want."

Her voice subdued with pain, Dora spoke into the flames of her punch glass.

"Give me to him."

Victor laughed.

"You silly child. Don't be cross. You needn't write a poem, even, and see? You may still have from me whatever you desire. Today, I feel like a king!"

"Swear it!"

"I swear it!"

Upon hearing these words, Dora sprang to her feet, upsetting the flaming punch. She made for Phryne. She pulled the longest tortoise shell pin from her yellow hair. The canvas screeched twice – a screech like that of a fairy in hell. And Dora stabbed out Phryne's eyes, the loveliest eyes on earth. And as the rising autumn sun poured the most splendid brightness of any of its mornings through the open window, true happiness lost its life's blood before its appointed time.

1905

The Wild Boy

Where on jingling sleighs reckless Russian gentlemen, many-rubelled and hungry for a kiss, flock to town for the girls and the bright lights, that is where Barbara longed to go. Away, away from beggarly Budapest, heartless and miserly with its magnificent women so splendid of shape. The news had reached her from legendary Moscow: the silken, Smirna berugged, perfumed *séparés* were waiting for women whose blood was of Tokay wine. All they had to do was sing, all they had to do was dance, and their neat little slippers were stuffed with thousand-rubel bank notes. And if they were light-hearted besides, the fancy, foolish gentlemen of the jingling sleighs showered them with diamonds. ("Why stay here?" Barbara thought. "To fire the hearts of bank clerks with lean wallets? Or be shameless for the frugal largesse of some aged and hateful count? To play on the keyboard of a typesetting machine and stand by as every monkey in the place tries to lay claim to my kisses? To be wed to the upright neighbourhood tradesman? It's high time I left," Barbara said as she worried her little head.)

In short, Barbara made up her mind to go. She set out, though with her went her listless, unsettling cares. ("Barbara, Barbara, you were born in a village, remember? A small Transylvanian village. Before your father and mother, none of your kind had ever even seen a big town. And even they came up to Pest with heavy hearts. Your mother was a housewife celebrated throughout seven counties. And both your grandmothers, too. And they all loved children. You had nine brothers and sisters yourself. *'Hush, little baby…'* Do you remember how you loved to lull the little ones to sleep? And now, you're off to Moscow. To Moscow.")

Barbara stamped her feet. She glanced out the window of the velvet-lined compartment of the express. With her white hand she smoothed down her brow and hair. She tried to chase the listless, unsettling cares away. ("I will not be a pauper! I am very beautiful. I can see. I can tell. Besides, what's to prevent me from bringing my youth back home if I wish? I shall bring it back, yes, I shall!")

Her bosom heaved, her magnificent hips trembled, her cheeks were set on fire. And as she promised herself the distant future, the immediate she tried to make more appealing. And on a white December night, she reached the rubelled city.

But that was a long time ago. After a while Barbara left the city where Russian gentlemen flocked, reckless and hungry for a kiss, where they flocked on jingling sleighs on wintry nights, sweeping over snow-clad plains. She heard the Caucasian musicians' noisy revel, to which she had danced so fiercely once, as if through a glass darkly. She had travelled extensively; she had been every-where, except Budapest. Her heart throbbed more, and her cheeks were less apt to burn. It might even kill her, she reasoned, were she to visit the old places where her two grandmothers had been celebrated housewives throughout seven counties, and where her mother had sung ten children to sleep. Oh, when Barbara thought of these things, her sick and unruly heart forced tears from her eyes larger than her diamonds. She'd go home gladly, she'd even die without a word, she felt. But she had to go on living for the sake of someone to whom she would soon make herself known. ("My precious torment, blood of my blood, I am your mother. I have come for you. I have come to take you away and make you a prince. You shall be fabulously wealthy. You do want to be fabulously wealthy, don't you? See? It is with you that life has blessed and cursed me.")

Yet Barbara put off visiting the boy Gábor, whom she had confined to the care of a tidy, upright Russian woman seven years before. She had taken a lawyer along at the time, and it was through him that she spoke. "I am a Hungarian countess. You shall bring up my son. You shall receive a handsome allowance for him. Love him, and take good care of him." And after that, the handsome allowance reached the child Gábor's nurse from sundry parts of the world. The lawyer, too, wrote regularly. "The child," he wrote, "is handsome and healthy. He is loved, he is being looked after."

("No. No. Not yet," thought Barbara. "I am afraid to go. The trip would kill me. I shall wait another spring before I go to fetch him, fetch my blessed adversity. Till then, let his money grow. It is his money. I have saved it for him. But I shall bring him away once. I shall take him home to Budapest. With him by my side, I am not afraid to go back home.")

And this is how the springs came and went, and the eighth arrived. And on the Riviera, in Cimiez,* in a fabulous villa adorned with a hundred different flowers, Barbara was stricken with a mother's longing, and her heart was more worn out and unruly than ever. ("The time has come for me to fetch you, my little son. I shall come and fetch you now. I have had enough. I have suffered enough. It is up to you now to cure me. I am coming for you, my precious transgression.")

Her doctor, too, had been incautious. Out on the terrace, he had said to the maid too loud, "Take good care of your mistress, Aimée. If all goes well, she may live another two months. Two months on the outside."

And Barbara heard him. She heard him. With a scream, she fainted. But as she swooned, a fiery

*Cimiez, the north-eastern suburb of Nice, was where the wealthiest guests stayed on the Riviera.

strength ignited her soul. It must not happen. It is not yet time. Mighty laws forbid that her heart should stop beating now. And the fate that destines certain women for motherhood and a mother's martyrdom appeared and settled itself upon the pale, bad-hearted mistress of the villa in Cimiez. By nightfall she said, "Tomorrow we are leaving for Moscow." Her voice was barely audible, but her resolve was firm.

So she headed for the legendary, rubelled city once more, as her little son stood watch over her heart. ("Oh, if only I could be there already, if only I could already be there! Two months! My son will be mine for just two months. I had imagined it so very differently! He will be handsome, tall, and clever. But he will know nothing of the past life of his poor little ailing mother. We will live together, and he will be the solace of my days.")

In Moscow, everything was just as it had been. The perfumed *séparés* still needed light-hearted women, both old and new. Tho foolish, frivolous gentlemen of the jingling sleighs still squandered their fortunes on the singing and dancing maidens. Barbara went looking for her lawyer. He had died, poor man, months before. And he didn't even send word. So the child Gábor's poor mother set out for the small nearby town with no one but her maid.

They found the town, however, and they also found the upright Russian woman. And only then did Barbara realise that she could speak no Russian. The few words from the past she had since forgotten.

She tried to speak to the woman in all other languages. She laughed, wept, cooed. She folded her arms as if cradling a child. *"Hush, little baby..."*

The woman understood. She led the way, with Barbara trailing behind. They reached a small cow shed. Inside, a tiny lad in a big fur hat and home-made boots was pitching straw.

The Russian woman dragged the child forward. Barbara covered her squeamish, deathly-pale face with a scented handkerchief. The stench was abominable. But then she looked into the boy's eyes, miraculously like her own. The child was strong, ruddy, grand. At the sight of him, all of Barbara's passion for life burst from her.

"My son, my little son, my very own precious darling! Your mother has come for you!"

The boy, the half-wild child, was frightened by this fancy feminine wonder. Brandishing a dirty, four pronged pitchfork, he drew back. He said something in Russian. The tiny lad seemed very wrought. He was probably cursing.

But it was not this awful wildness that wrung Barbara's bad, ailing heart. It was the realization, newly come, that she could never communicate with her son, from whom she had expected her deliverance. And she had less than two months to live! If only she could kiss him! But the child shied away, lashing out with the dirty pitchfork.

Barbara succumbed without a sound. In vain did her maid attempt to revive her with perfumed essences. There was no life in her. The wild boy, too, was alarmed. He dropped the pitchfork, and they all leaned over Barbara. In the filthy stable, this fancy, lifeless woman was amazing. Her lips, especially. Mad, crazed and desperate, they were pursed for a kiss.

1905

Thomas in the Red Garden

Azuba sat in the red garden. It thundered, and a host of clouds descended from the sky. Night fell. The universe was in gloom. The host of clouds pressed great, suffocating perfumes against the earth. Azuba pinned a flower in her hair. She bedewed her violet eyes with fresh tears, and sang.

Outside the garden, on the edge of the olive grove, someone screamed. He screamed a horrible, wild scream. Then he headed for the garden, stumbling as he ran.

The thunder of the sky continued. The host of clouds brushed against the rosebushes. Wild, horrible screams broke forth from the womb of the earth, and once or twice the clouds blinked, and in their eyes burned the frightful fire of the sky.

He who had come from the olive grove collapsed, weeping, at Azuba's feet.

"Maiden of the red garden, oh, my sin of yesteryear, my beloved, it is I. Look at me, it is I, Thomas."

Seven-coloured tears trickled from Azuba's eyes as she sang.

"Azuba, Azuba, won't you look at me? You might as well look now, for we are all about to die. Earth and sky cannot hold. Let me die upon the taste of your honeyed kisses. Unworthy as I am, let your arms embrace me one last time."

The universe shuddered. The might of Creation boomed. A fiery, celestial flash dried up Azuba's violet eyes. She gazed at the man kneeling before her and, still singing, stood. She plucked roses from the red bushes. Then she spoke.

"So you have returned. Oh, I knew, I knew you would return. Why do you weep? Why do you tremble? You were so proud and triumphant just yesterday. You drove me from you to follow that other. Well, where is that other now? Why do you ask for my kisses?"

The man's voice faltered.

"They have killed the King of the Jews, the Prince of the World, the Son of God. I have just come from that place. It is stained with blood. The Master hangs upon the gallows-tree, flanked by thieves. Oh, Life will cease now, and so will the World. The Father of our King will have His revenge. Can't you see the awesome signs? Can't you hear the frightful rumblings? Kiss me, kiss me quickly, lest I die without a kiss."

Azuba's violet eyes sparkled.

"Oh, my faint-hearted beloved! What maddened words are these? You crave my kisses? Why, then, do you not drink your fill of them? For whom have I mourned since that man from Nazareth robbed me of you? For whom have I kept my fire and my kisses? For you, my beloved, while I withered away in this red garden and cursed him who took you from me. Is he dead? Hallelujah! Hallelujah! My curse bore fruit! For it was I cursed him, and my roses cursed him, him, the sad one, the unctuous one, the stranger, the evil one. Do not tremble! What do you see? It is evening. Can you smell the sweet perfume of my roses? The redness of my garden shimmers crimson in the night. From beyond the mountain, behold, the Moon is rising. And over there, the Evening Star. Oh, how often it did shine on our embraces! Now the world is still. There is nothing but the distant song of lovers. So he is on the gallows, there on the hill? Oh, blessed day! Oh, long night of love! Have you anything more to forget? What more would you forget?"

"Things aplenty. Kiss away my sadness with your kisses. You have gladdened the world now. I no longer hear that which is terrible, nor behold that which is fearful. What miracles you work, my beloved! But tell me, tell me that men are not unhappy, that life is resplendent with pleasure, that we must live for ourselves alone. Tell me that to kiss is no transgression, that the Roman soldiers are not executioners, that all scribes are not evil. Tell me that we need not remember that which we choose to forget, that all our gods are true, the red gardens truly red, and that Azuba is everything unto her Thomas."

"Kiss me, and kiss me again, and think not of the

kisses that have been kissed away. Kiss me and think not of yesteryear's sorrow. The red gardens are truly red, and Azuba is everything unto her Thomas. Oh, despair not, my beloved! My handmaiden has prepared sweetmeats and wine. They await us on our bed of roses. And now, may many dawns pursue each other, for my darling has not kissed me in many a day."

The sky's brilliance sparkled, and the groves poured forth their perfumes. The redness of the garden shimmered, and their kisses trilled, like the thrush, and in the meantime, the sun set thrice.

Then on one fine, delicate and fragrant night, Thomas stirred from a dream. His eyes gleamed crimson. He sat up on the bed of roses and screamed.

"Get Thee hence! They have killed Thee. Thou art dead. Get Thee from my sight!"

And Azuba began to sob with the evil forebodings of her heart.

"My beloved, are you weary? Have you grown weary of delight? Speak to me instead, for there is no one there. Oh, my, there is no one, no thing there!"

But Thomas continued to stare into the void, and his words were feverish.

"Thou art mercy incarnate. Thou wilt forgive Thy miserable servant, Lord. Thou art the Son of God, and they could not kill Thee, no! I have touched your wound with my finger. Oh, forgive those who doubt. Thou hast risen from the dead, King of Kings, while I, the vile slave of the body, have brought eternal damnation upon my head. I am weary and mortified. Lead me away, Lord, that I may give solace to the world."

"Thomas! Thomas!"

Azuba sobbed, and in a wild agony of grief, clutched her lover's shoulder. And behold, a turbulent night descended. The air grew thick with monsters. A chorus of woeful evening hymns ascended to the sky. The roses began to fade, and the red garden to turn white, and Thomas, he ran out into the night.

From time to time, a sharp, whistling wind brought back his shrill cries.

"Hallelujah! Hallelujah! Rejoice!"

Azuba stood in the night, staring after him. Her lovely, feverish body trembled. Then a mad, demonic laugh broke from her lips. She tore the rose from her hair, the last red rose of the garden, and flung it away.

1905

.

Printed in Hungary, 1994